Love in the Afterlife

Ashlyn Chase

Content warning: Some graphic love scenes, and language. Okay, more than some. Lots. Lots and lots.

Trigger warning: Suicide scene

The ultimate in human soul recycling.

When Heather Tripp hobbles on crutches into her boring insurance job in Atlanta on a leap day morning, she never expects to crash into an alternate realm or meet the two immortals in charge of death and reincarnation.

Blaze Stevens, a delivery driver by day, rock band drummer by night, has no idea he's responsible for the two of them plummeting down an elevator shaft, into this alternate realm.

Without knowing if they are dead or alive, the two of them cling to their tentative reality, and each other, while they figure out if and how they can get back home. They sure as hell aren't in Atlanta, or even Kansas, anymore.

CHAPTER ONE

Heather Tripp was sick of her virginity. It was time to lose it and she had decided that the next decent-looking guy who tried to get into her pants was going to get lucky—even if she did have a broken leg.

"Stop—wait!" yelled a deep voice from across the broad Atlanta, Georgia, street.

Heather nearly wrenched her back as she turned to see who was shouting. Her cast and crutches firmly anchored the rest of her body in front of a revolving door leading into the Phoenix Insurance Corp. building. Peering through her fluttering strands of brown hair, about to frizz in the Hotlanta humidity, she spotted the guy who had sounded like he was panicking. A magnificent, exotic looker, wearing a black leather jacket and just-right, tight jeans, caught up with her and opened the side delivery door.

"You'll get mangled going through that revolving thing on crutches. It looks like we're heading into the same building. The least I can do is hold the door for you."

"Thanks." She limped over to the door as a gust of wind caught the hem of her short, tulip skirt. Without a free hand to hold it down she may as well be putting on a burlesque show—not that she didn't want to gain the attention of the gorgeous hunk standing there, but some other way would have been nice. The heat in her cheeks signaled she was blushing.

Heather gulped when he passed her, sporting a roguish smile. He stepped into the elevator and held the doors open while she hopped along as fast as she could on crutches and one foot. And to think, if her injury hadn't slowed her down today, she might have missed him. Heather resented her unfortunate plunge off the stage at the Miss Peaches and Cream pageant a little less.

As they silently rode the elevator together, she couldn't help glancing up at him a few times. He had gorgeous raven hair, unruly and curling around his jacket collar. His hand tucked in one pocket said he was casual, but self-assured. Unable to resist, she leaned back and took a quick peek at his ass. *Yummy.* When he smiled down at her and winked one of his chocolate-brown eyes, her heart stopped. Was that a wink or a tic? God, she hoped it wasn't a tic. If only it took longer to reach the twenty-ninth floor.

When the doors didn't open to the bustling office, she didn't even notice. Mmm. He smelled like leather and musky male. She wanted to stand near him in an enclosed space all day and fill her nostrils with his scent.

If I could choose anyone to take my virginity...

Before she had a chance to think of something to talk about, she heard a metallic squeal. The elevator dropped a few inches and bounced. A sick feeling roiled her stomach. She and Blaze stared at each other, wide-eyed. Suddenly something let go and the elevator dropped like a rock.

They screamed in unison as their plunge toward doom accelerated. The numbers above the door flashed in quick succession, signifying the floors as they passed. In no time they were in single digits. Heather watched, frozen in helpless panic. Seven, six, five, four, three, two, one...

She screamed, "Fuck," scrunched her eyes shut and braced for the inevitable impact. Oddly enough, they didn't stop falling.

"Hey! We're not landing!" Blaze shouted.

Gawking at the numbers, Heather couldn't believe what she saw. *Negative nine, negative ten, negative eleven...*

Blaze began counting out loud. "Negative eighteen? Negative nineteen? Negative twenty?"

The elevator slowed and both of them had their eyes glued to the numbers, chanting in unison. "Negative twenty-seven—negative twenty-eight—negative twenty-nine..."

The number sequence stopped, as did the elevator, heralding the end of their traumatic descent.

Blaze's large eyes stared at her. "Are we dead? Did we go to—?" The doors whooshed open, cutting off his question.

Damp fingers of fog reached into the elevator as a preternatural scene greeted Heather's astonished gaze. An eerie, blue-green light permeated the billowing fog, peeking through thin spots. A pond beneath the miasma seemed to be emitting a strange, iridescent illumination.

They both hesitated but eventually each one of them stepped out onto wet grass and gazed at their mystifying surroundings. Heather, hobbling, followed close behind Blaze. Spanish moss hung from giant trees, gnarled, and twisted with age. Weird, otherworldly noises, like mournful birds, cried in the distance. The smell of wet moss hung in the air. Soon the fog dissipated. It appeared to be early morning, just before dawn. The sky was the color of Blaze's indigo jeans.

Oh Lord. She couldn't believe she was thinking of his jeans at a time like this, but he had been walking in front of her and she couldn't help admiring...

A figure dressed in a flowing, brown robe, stood with its back to them on the opposite side of the pond. Platinum hair cascaded down the creature's back. It seemed to be made of flax, not that Heather really knew what that was. Maybe the correct term was flaxen hair? Whenever she got confused, she wound up babbling in her head, exactly as she was doing now. *Get a grip, Tripp.*

Then the elevator disappeared. *What the hell is going on?*

Blaze called out in the direction of the stranger across the pond. "Hey, you! Where are we?"

Startled he'd talk to an unknown person, or entity, in a freakish environment, Heather wondered what was wrong with guy? Still, they had to ask someone where they were. Deciding to respect his assertiveness and ability to take charge, she just prayed the natives were friendly.

The figure didn't turn around. Instead, a low voice began to hum. The hum grew louder and at last evolved into the sound of a female singing a tune; a song that seemed to resonate from everywhere and nowhere.

*"'Where am I? Where am I?' That's what you're thinking.
Traveled somewhere without even blinking.
Am I in Heaven? Am I on Earth?
Traveled in time to before my own birth?
Such silly mortals with mortalish thoughts.
Wondering now if you've had all your shots."*

Resuming her hum, she turned around to face them. She tipped her head to the right, then to the left, and appeared to be studying them.

As if annoyed at having been disturbed, she jammed her hands on her hips and sang again.

> *"Picture a moment; a place beyond dreams*
> *That's waterfall fresh with candy sweet scenes.*
> *That's not where you've landed, and though I'm your host,*
> *I am an immortal, so almost a ghost."*

Heather trembled and clumsily grabbed hold of Blaze's leather jacket. The stranger laughed out loud, and her song turned into a shout.

> *"No, you're not dead, though that can be arranged.*
> *You're saving your souls! You're here to be changed!"*

After the last verse, the odd woman disappeared in a puff of smoke. In the blink of Heather's tear-filled eyes, the figure reappeared directly in front of her. She shook so hard she dropped her crutches. Trying to back away, but trapped by her clunky cast, she stumbled and landed on her butt in the soft moss. "Blaze, run!"

"Aww...fell on your tush, did you?" the whatever-she-was said. "Hmm. Nice white skirt you're wearing. That'll leave a stain."

"This can't be happening." Blaze bent to pick up her crutches and whispered, "I won't leave you."

Heather took one look at his determined expression and swallowed hard. He reached under her arm and helped her up.

The warm strength of him seeped into her. She wanted to hang onto him until she stopped shivering. He could almost distract her from this craziness. *That's it! I must be at my desk—going crazy. I fell asleep from utter boredom. Any minute now, I'll wake up.*

Meanwhile, the peculiar woman paced back and forth in front of them, looking them over from top to bottom.

"You're from the Earthly realm. You were wise to seek me out, although I must say I'm amazed you found me. It was decided long ago that I should remain hidden from you."

She sighed and began to sit. A chair appeared underneath her by the time she needed it, thus preventing her from falling on her ass. Heather wished she had plummeted to the ground. Maybe a little humor would make her laugh and wake her up out of this dream.

A very long, metal spoon appeared in the woman's hand, and she pointed it at Heather. "Hey, watch that. I'll be the one to decide what happens to whom."

Heather caught her breath. Did she just read my mind? A moment later, a stream of small rocks fell from the sky and plopped into the water. Concentric circles emanated from the spots where the pebbles had disturbed the placid surface. *Why the hell are stones falling from the sky into a neon pond? Moreover, who is this strange creature pointing a two-foot-long metal spoon at me as if it were a magic wand?*

CHAPTER TWO

"Oh, that's right," said the singing Dr. Seuss. "You don't know who I am. I guess I'll have to introduce myself." She tossed her head and crossed her legs, the robe falling open to reveal their shapeliness. "I have many different names, but you can call me Tophet."

After a period of silence, she sighed. "For heaven's sake, will one of you please get over your speechless panic and talk to me? Do you know how long it's been since I've heard another voice? Not that I don't love the sound of my own voice, I do, but come on... Speak!"

"You can hear what we're thinking?" Blaze asked.

"Yes. By the way, thanks for the compliment on my legs, but they're not really a mile long."

His jaw dropped and he took a giant step backward. Blaze managed to straighten his posture and cross his arms in front of his chest. "Okay, what was I just thinking?"

Tophet chuckled. "Your mind was blank. Your brain is still frozen in fear, although you're doing an impressive job of hiding your terror." She waved them over and gestured to the grass at her feet. "Come. Sit down. I won't bite."

Heather took a deep breath and hoped it was true. As they settled on the ground, Blaze happened to lay the boomerang-shaped bone on the grass in front of Tophet.

"My boomerang! Where did you find it?"

Neither one answered for a moment. At last, Blaze wiped the sweat from his brow and whispered an answer. "It was in the package I was supposed to deliver to the Paleontology Department."

She walked past them and asked, "What day is it in your world?"

Heather cleared her throat and squeaked a reply. "Monday, February 29th."

"Leap Day? Oh, no!" The immortal slapped her hand over her eyes. "The chink in time's armor. You must go back today, or you'll be stranded here. I'll be stuck with you for four years—like a bad administration."

Heather gulped. "Stranded here? Oh my God!" Even with a handsome stranger... *Oh my God!* Heather couldn't speak. Not another word would come out of her dry throat. She wanted her mommy.

Tophet closed her eyes and massaged her temples. "Okay, don't panic. Let's see. How can you get out of here?"

Heather and Blaze looked at each other and shrugged.

"Oh, this is just fabulously horrible. You don't know how to return to your own realm?"

They shook their heads.

Tophet frowned and stuck her hands on her hips. "All right. I'll have to figure it out myself. In the meantime, what can you do to help me in exchange for putting up with you?"

Blaze's brow furrowed. "What do you mean?"

"I mean, do you have any skills? What do you do in your world that you might be able to do for me while I'm busy solving your problem for you?"

Heather piped up. "I can type and file."

Tophet stared at her in silence for a moment. "Young lady, do you see anything to type on or any folders to file?"

Heather shook her head.

Blaze raised his hand. "I can play the drums. Maybe I could find some sticks in the woods and—"

"And what? Drive me out of my gourd with mind-numbing, meaningless clatter?"

"Oh, I can make coffee! Good coffee," Heather offered. "Do you have a coffee pot?"

Tophet brightened. "Now you're talking. There's an espresso machine right over there." She waved her spoon and a small coffee bar appeared. "Keep the pot fresh, full, and strong. That's the way I like it."

More rocks and pebbles crashed down from the sky. Tophet whirled toward the pond and shouted, "I'll get there when I'm good and ready!" Just as quickly as her attention had been diverted, she jerked her focus back to Heather. "Where's that coffee?"

Heather hurried to the coffee bar and prepared the hot espresso. The fragrance of coffee brewing helped drown out the swampy smell of the pond.

Blaze leaned forward. "What exactly did you mean when you said we could be stranded here?"

Tophet's posture slumped. "Yes. This is my fault I'm afraid. But I hate to take the blame, if there's any way around it. I have another dilemma you might help me with. Want to hear it?"

Heather returned to her spot beside Blaze, and they grasped each other's hands.

Tophet shook her head at them. "Whatever…it'll be good to get it off my chest. So, like it or not, here it comes." She glowered and paced. "I've been the keeper of the Pond of Souls for all eternity, literally, and I've never seen so many dried-up little turds of souls returning at once!"

She faced the pond and raised her arms. The fabric of her earth-colored robe flapped in the breeze, making her appear to glide.

Wait a minute. She *was* gliding, kind of floating toward the glowing water.

"It's as if none of them are reaching the next level. I don't think they're even trying anymore. Even Gandhi's in there. I thought for sure he was moving up. He seemed to have the concept." She folded her arms and shook her head.

"Now you're here, and I'm beginning to think something is definitely out of whack." She grabbed a cup of coffee and disappeared with a light poof. When the smoke cleared, she was standing on the other side of the pond, where she had been when they first arrived.

CHAPTER THREE

Heather let out the breath she'd been holding, relieved to have some distance between them. Suddenly a bright light, like an old-fashioned camera, flashed and blinded her for a second. Her heart lurched. When the billowing smoke that surrounded them cleared and she could see again, she and Blaze were standing next to Tophet. To make matters worse, Tophet was standing next to a cauldron.

What now? Cannibalism?

The immortal shook her head. "Ick, that doesn't sound very appetizing to me. I'll have to find another way to dispose of—that is, I mean, deal with you. Meanwhile, listen up. There's another quandary I want to discuss. That's the one you might be able to help with. Gather round."

They obediently positioned themselves between Tophet and the cauldron. Blaze crossed and uncrossed his arms. He leaned on one hip and then the other, and generally did lots of fidgeting.

"For the love of beef jerky, will you two please relax? I won't kill you. I don't do Death's job for him, and he doesn't do mine for me."

Blaze cleared his throat. "Um...then what do you want us to do?"

"Ah, thank you, Mortal Number One. Remember when I said, 'It might be my fault'?" Tophet's long metal spoon appeared in her hand again and she used it to point at him.

He jumped backward but eventually answered with a hesitant, "Yes."

"Well, I'm bored silly and barely paying attention to my work anymore. I may have been lax in protecting my whereabouts. I know I've been lax in production and distribution. I've even been lax in relaxing. I've been lax in everything!

"Mortal Number One, I notice you curse a lot—in your head. I've tried to entertain myself by coming up with a new expletive. All the best ones are religious in nature: 'What the Hell; God Damnit; Jesus Christ...' I can't use any of those. I'm strictly nonsectarian and nondenominational. You see what I'm up against?"

More rocks bombarded the pond. A small amount of water splashed onto Tophet's robe and her face turned red. She visibly shook before discharging a deafening shout. "Gaaah!" Looking down, she noticed she had spilled coffee on her robe too. She took several deep breaths and yelled again.

"See what I mean? Frustration is mounting. I need the immediate release of some new profanity. The old expressions have lost their satisfaction and nothing new seems to be coming to me."

Blaze folded his muscular arms across his broad chest and said, "All stressed up and no one to choke, huh?"

Heather elbowed him in the ribs. When he looked at her and shrugged, she shook her head. It didn't matter. Caution probably wouldn't save their lives and she still wanted to hand him her virginity on a platter.

"Come on Mortal Number One, I know you can do this."

Blaze scuffed the ground and mumbled, "This is bullshit."

"What's that?" Tophet asked. "A suggestion? Colorful, but it somewhat reminds me of the problem that started this whole spiraling cycle of angst in the first place. You know those dried up little excreted globules of souls constantly falling into my pond? They remind me of poop. They muck up my pond and consume all my time. Think about it, though. You're on the right track."

Tophet resumed her pacing and sipped her coffee. "It has to be larger than life. A swear to dwarf all swears." Ceasing her strut, she whipped around and glared at them both. "You're kidding. Did one of you just suggest the word 'fuck'? You know, I never could understand that one. Why don't we all just stand in the middle of a sunny, daisy-covered meadow and yell *Pleasure*? Or when you want to swear at someone else, 'Pleasure yourself'!"

Heather had a hard time holding back her giggle.

Tophet dropped the metal spoon in the cauldron and marched back and forth in front of them, shaking her head. "The word is overused and not very fulfilling anymore. Almost everyone uses that one at some point, even good little girlie here. I need something original." She abruptly stopped her pacing and focused on Heather. With a sarcastic expression on her face, she asked, "Are you old enough to hear the word 'fuck' Mortal Number Two?"

Since the all-powerful one seemed ticked off at the moment, Heather went mute again and simply nodded.

Tophet picked up the spoon and wagged it at her as if it were an elongated index finger. "I took pity on you two as you fell because one of you shouted out your fondest, unfulfilled wish, and that was it. It may have sounded like a swear, but I knew better. I couldn't let it go unanswered." She stared at Heather. "You understand, don't you?"

Heather did. *Oh fuck.*

Tophet waited while the couple looked at the sky, the pond, anything but each other.

"No one wants to own up to it. Well then, fuck it." Tophet dropped into a lounge chair that materialized under her butt just in time.

Blaze's forehead furrowed, as if momentarily confused. Then he turned his widened eyes to stare at a rapidly reddening Heather. "Oh!"

Tophet let out a deep sigh and draped her arm over the back of the chair. "But enough about you. Now think mortals, think! If I can release my frustration, I may be able to concentrate on a way to send you home. If I can't, you may have plenty of time to come up with a variety of expressions. Living with me for the next four years won't be easy, with or without each other for company. I'm no day at the lake when I'm all stressed up." She glowered at Blaze.

CHAPTER FOUR

Tophet yawned. "I'd better get back to my utterly boring, routine job, which I can't stand another moment." She downed the rest of her coffee. "You don't mind if I work and talk at the same time, do you?"

She stared at Heather and said, "Of course I can work and talk at the same time, Mortal Number Two. I'm an omnipotent immortal."

This mind-reading stuff is getting outrageous.

Tophet shrugged, dipped her spoon into the cauldron and lifted out a generous helping of a glowing, green, gelatinous substance. Heather's stomach churned and her head began to whirl. *Dear God, she isn't going to make us eat it, is she?*

The all-knowing one turned to face them and let out a laugh that turned into a cackle. As she held her stomach, trying to catch her breath in between whoops of laughter, the jiggling, radioactive looking Jell-O slipped off the spoon and plopped back into the cauldron.

"Oops. Sorry. Dropped you on your little head, did I?" She snickered and scooped up the glob with her hand. Patting and shaping it, she said, "There, you poor soul, you'll be as good as new. Wait a minute..." She examined the gel from every angle and spoke to it again. "Not *you*. Do you really think you're ready to go back and try again?"

She held the glob to her ear and then looked over at the curious duo. "He said he's learned his lesson. Well, we'll see." She leaned back and hurled the handful of ooze as if she were pitching for the Atlanta Braves.

"Humph. Some souls have a habit of returning too frequently due to their own foolhardiness. It annoys me."

Tophet paced back and forth with the spoon dangling at her side, dripping a wet, green trail behind her. "As if I don't have enough work..." She shook her fist at the void that had swallowed the ball of goop. "I hope the Indians in that rainforest teach you something, like listening when you're specifically told, 'Don't try this at home'!"

The inadvertent visitors gazed at each other with alarm. Heather's heart started to pound, and this time it wasn't due to Blaze.

Tophet dipped her spoon into the vat again and Blaze spoke up. "Do you mean to tell us these little, green globs are souls, and you decide what lives these souls will come back to—like reincarnation?"

Tophet rolled her eyes. "It's not *like* reincarnation Mortal Number One, it *is* reincarnation!" She touched the jiggling soul with her index finger. "What have we here? Oh, you think you've got a shot at fame this time? Probably..." She did a wind up and a pitch. "Not!" The green, glowing ball disappeared over the trees.

Heather gasped.

"Get over it, Mortal Number Two. He was an actor and as arrogant as they come. Thought he could make it on his looks alone. He wasn't interested in learning from directors or more experienced actors in order to do his best. Therefore, he must repeat his lesson until it's learned. I just sent him to Los Angeles, but he'll grow up to become an attorney. At least he'll have plenty of opportunities to polish his acting skills."

More rocks poured into the pond and Tophet cringed. "Have either of you come up with that perfect curse word yet? I'm still waiting for that power-packed tension reliever."

Heather screwed up her courage, but not to suggest the perfect profanity. She thought she might try softening the immortal with sympathy. "I wish I had an Aspirin for you. It must be hard to decide peoples' fates. I know it would give me a headache."

Tophet dropped into her chair. "Hard to decide peoples' fates? No, not at all, Mortal Number Two, but thanks for trying to make me feel better. People decide their own fates. Usually, the next incarnation is obvious. It's up to me to give them a fighting chance to learn the appropriate lessons and eventually move on to a higher plane."

Blaze chimed in. "You know, I've always found the idea of reincarnation fascinating."

"Fascinating? Mortal Number One thinks this is fascinating." Tophet leaned back against her chair, closed her eyes, and draped an arm across her forehead like a drama queen. She groaned, inhaled deeply, then shouted, "I am so bored!" Bored, bored, ord, or...

A long, charged silence followed the echo. Heather and Blaze glanced at their surroundings, wondering about the unlikely echo.

There were no canyons in view, just the forest and a mountain range, the color of a blue and purple bruise with snowy peaks, far off in the distance. Tophet straightened up and glared at them. "It's the same routine, day after massively dull day, for eternity. Insert expletive here."

Heather shook her head and said, "Geezum Crow, I know what you mean. That's just like my job at the insurance company."

Tophet raised her eyebrows. "Mortal Number Two, that was pathetic. Nevertheless, until I can find something better, I'll just have to resort to weakly-worded outbursts. Can you understand why a good, furious curse word might help? Don't y'all let one slip once in a while when you're really angry, little Miss Well-Bred-Beauty-Queen?"

"I was taught not to swear at all. My mother was grooming me for Miss Georgia. I had made it to the finals in the 'Miss Peaches and Cream' pageant and then I fell off the stage during my dance number and broke my leg."

"Well, hobble on over to the coffee bar and make me another cup of this." She waved her spoon at the coffee bar on the opposite side of the pond, then *poofed* it to the empty patch of grass next to Heather. "Stronger this time."

"Yes Ma'am."

"Don't call me Ma'am! I hate that. It makes me feel old."

Heather responded without thinking. "But you *are* old, aren't you?"

Tophet leaped out of her chair and glared at her, making her quiver all over like a Jell-O mold or a soul on a spoon.

Blaze inserted his body between them and yelled, "Leave her alone. You *are* old, just like she said. For God's sake, you're a fuckin' immortal! You know what's really pathetic? With all the powers you have, you can't think of a single thing to do that you can be passionate about. I'm a drummer in a rock band when I'm not delivering packages to pencil-pushers. Eventually, I'll be part of a famous band, making recordings, touring and shit. But if we were stuck here, I'd reach into that pond and pull out some in-fuckin'-credible musicians like Hendrix or Morrison, and I'd be making awesome music with the most fan-fucking-tastic bands while I did my fuck-ass, boring job. And *you* need us to entertain you? That's pa-fucking-thetic."

Heather was sure Blaze was toast, but Tophet just scratched her head and sighed.

"Your point is well taken, kid. Some type of entertainment might help alleviate the monotony." Her eyes narrowed into slits and the powerful immortal frowned until a glint of mischief appeared on her face.

Heather felt a shiver run down her spine and she grabbed Blaze's hand.

CHAPTER FIVE

Okay, kids. I've thought of a way to entertain myself and you'll never know what hit you.

Blaze tried again. "How about another swear—I've got it. How about 'May a stink bug fart in your eye'? Something like that?"

Tophet nodded, giving the appearance of considering the suggestion, but she was more interested in implementing her wicked plan. It was time to make these two odd strangers a bit more fascinating—at least to each other. It might be downright fan-fucking-tastic to watch live porn. She'd simply make them fall madly in love with each other, instantly. Easy!

"Keep trying to come up with those curse words and expressions. We'll need to think of some more. Now I must get back to work." She tapped the side of the cauldron. "Yeah, this is a good batch. Be quiet for a few minutes, I need to do some magic."

She peered into the cauldron and when she knew the mortals were giving her their full attention, she snapped her head up and pointed her metal spoon at them.

Declare your love and run for cover,
Or I will see you boink your lover!

The smoke that ensued was thicker than usual. When it finally cleared, Heather and Blaze were pressed into each other's arms, fervently kissing. Their embrace was so tight it seemed as if they were welded together. Their passion increased until it was smoldering, literally. Some of the smoke either didn't clear, or it was pouring off the two of them.

"Oh my!" Tophet said. "I think you'd better listen to my advice and hide before I have to watch you boffing each other senseless." The two of them paid no attention to her. "Please, I insist you go have fun. I'll be waiting for you right here."

They broke their lip-lock long enough for Blaze to scoop Heather up, cast and all. As he spirited her away, Tophet chuckled under her breath and muttered, "Don't worry. I'll be entertained...especially since I'm clair-voyeur-ant." She reared her head back and laughed out loud.

Sensing their wild, beating hearts, Tophet knew they were both frightened by what they had just been about to do right in front of a stranger, yet at the same time, utterly turned-on and enslaved by their uncontrollable passion. Tophet couldn't have been more pleased.

Blaze, carrying Heather, sprinted into the brush on the edge of the dense forest. Tophet called out, "There's a nice grotto in there. Just go straight ahead." She watched, amused, as Heather gave her the thumbs up.

***

Surrounded by tall shady trees, admiring the perfect circle carpeted with thick grass, Blaze dropped to his knees and gently set Heather down on what seemed like a soft, putting green.

"My love," he said. "I'm going to make a woman of you."

Floating above the couple, unbeknownst to them, Tophet's chair stretched into a chaise lounge. She reclined on it as if she were Cleopatra.

The young couple leaned toward one another reverently. Blaze trailed his fingers down Heather's arm, tender and slow. He cupped her face and drew her lips to his. The soft kiss expanded. He teased her lips with his tongue until she opened to him and then slanted his mouth over hers to deepen the kiss. Soon their lips were fused. They kissed passionately until Heather became aware of the need to breathe. They allowed their lips to draw apart, both of them panting. She sighed when he began to remove her clothing.

While all of this was happening, Tophet immersed herself deep in the scene as if she were actually Heather, feeling all of her hormonal reactions and over-stimulation as the young virgin experienced intimacy for the first time.

Blaze slid the zipper down Heather's back and the cool breeze added to her shivering anticipation. Her nipples puckered into sensitive peaks. He slid the fabric up and over his lover's head. The material drew up her body like a stage curtain, along with the incredible anticipation of sex, excited her raw nerve endings and she crackled with electricity, hungry for more.

Tophet lost herself in the girl, experiencing every snap, crackle, and pop, as if they were under the same skin. *Oh, yes...I haven't felt like this for millennia.*

Heather raised her body by bracing her arms behind her as he slipped her skirt's elastic waist over her hips and down her thighs. Gently, he lifted her cast while she drew back her good leg and he removed the skirt completely. She sat in front of him, exposed except for her white, cotton underwear. Blaze paused. His eyes swept over her body, and he smiled.

"I love your body. I can't wait to make love to you. I promise I'll be gentle. Don't be afraid."

In a husky voice, sounding like a breathy attempt at seduction and at the same time feeling like a model for Innocent Magazine, she answered, "I'm not. I want you more than you know."

Blaze eased his leather jacket off his shoulders and removed it. As soon as it was carelessly tossed to the side, he scooted closer to Heather. She reached for the gray t-shirt that covered his muscled chest and purred as she ran her hands over his rippled abs. He was so taut and masculine. She could picture him in one of those sexy calendars. Her fingers stilled and she looked up at him in alarm. "Are you dating anyone?"

"No."

Her brow furrowed. "Why not? You're gorgeous."

"Thanks. You're awfully pretty too. But to answer your question, I'm not dating anybody, because I haven't found the one for me. I don't want the types of girls I meet at my rock concerts. I guess underneath it all, I kind of want a traditional girl."

"What about girls you could be meeting in other places?"

"Well, I looked at on-line dating, but I didn't know how to fill out the questionnaire when I got to the question about race. I'm White, Hispanic, African American, and Native American. I didn't know which box to check. I didn't want to upset anybody."

Heather chuckled. "Don't worry. It doesn't bother me if you're every flavor on the Ben and Jerry's menu. If you shake my family tree hard enough, one or two other races are bound to fall out."

She continued running her hands over his t-shirt. "Oh Blaze, I never knew a man's chest could be so strong and hard."

He took her hands and slipped them underneath the jersey fabric.

As she felt his body, Blaze watched her and smiled. When her hands eventually traveled back to the bottom of his shirt, she pulled it over his head. He raised his arms to help her. After she had taken a full appreciative appraisal of Blaze's muscled torso, she reached slowly for her shoulder straps and lowered her white bra. At the sight of her naked upper body, Blaze's breath audibly hitched in his throat.

After several seconds of Blaze staring at Heather's bare breasts as if he had never seen any before, Tophet popped out of Heather's body and resumed her view from the lounge above them.

"What's that goober doing?" she muttered under her breath. "It's not like he's never seen breasts before. They aren't even that impressive." She had hoped these two would make stimulating viewing but she was losing interest...and becoming *bored!*

What went wrong? "Oh, moose barf. I used the word 'love', didn't I?"

They'd be staring into each other's eyes, treating each other respectfully and taking their damn time all afternoon. If they didn't fornicate soon, she was going to have to play with herself.

"Silly mortals."

"Oooh..." Blaze was touching Heather's breasts. Finally! Tophet stroked her own breasts, groaning and catching her breath each time he grazed Heather's nipples. She felt his touch with the same powerful charge of the highly hormonal female. Then he leaned down and suckled her breasts, exploring the rest of Heather's body with his enthusiastic hands.

Tophet rode along as Heather braced herself on the cool grass, shivered and reared back with rippling sensations in her womb.

"Ohh." The pleasant suction on her breasts set her quivering. Blaze suckled deeper, taking more of Heather's breast into his mouth, flicking his tongue over her nipple. Glorious clenching sensations rocked her feminine core. "Oh, my."

Tophet hoped the poor girl didn't pass out.

As he moved his hand down, slipping it under her panties, Heather's legs shook. Tophet mirrored the girl's every move and reacted at exactly the same moments. She felt the moisture between her legs, wet with barely controlled anticipation. She almost laughed out loud when she thought about the little mortal's well-earned title—Miss Peaches and Cream. The sexy meaning. When at last Blaze fingered Heather's clitoris, both women gasped, arching their backs.

"Oh, my goodness!" Heather cried.

Blaze massaged her clit, stroking her into a burning fever as he nibbled and suckled each of her outthrust breasts. With one skillful flick of his thumb, Heather bucked, trembled, and screamed in ecstasy. "Yes, yes. Oh, my goodness, yes!"

Tophet silently screamed her release, as if she had turned off the volume. Good thing since she used more colorful language.

Slowly drawing her back from her climax, Blaze continued kissing and fondling Heather until she had recovered, and then he resumed suckling her breasts and massaging her oversensitive mons. She shuddered and trembled with the aftershocks, swaying so much she almost toppled over. He held her until she was steady and then helped her lie down on the grass.

"Heather, my love, are you sure you're ready for this?"

"I—I think so. I don't know. Maybe we could talk for a while?"

"All right."

Tophet sat up and silently shouted, "No!" She blew out a long breath of disgust. *I can't believe they stopped—to talk!*

She shook her head in resignation and popped back to the cauldron to resume her work—frustrated to the brink of insanity. It was a good thing she had some time to calm down.

Forty-two souls later, the two sweaty lovers emerged from the woods and collapsed in front of Tophet, grinning like giddy teenagers.

Blaze kissed Heather and tried to get to second base right in front of their hostess. Heather pulled away and playfully slapped Blaze's hand.

Tophet straightened her back and stared at them. "You two finally did it, didn't you?"

Heather giggled.

Phooey, I missed it.

CHAPTER SIX

Tophet closed her eyes. Her chaise lounge appeared underneath her just before she stretched out and laid down. She went into a deep, instant-replay trance and let the erotic sensations Heather had experienced happen to her. She had fast-forwarded through the talking part and replayed what she wanted. Ah, yes. She shivered with anticipation and writhed when the familiar sensations of lips and fingers touching and poking coursed through her.

A few seconds later she heard Blaze speak. "Hi there. What are you doing, you sexy immortal, you?"

"I'm knitting a blanket; what does it look like I'm doing?" she snapped.

"Well, it looks like you need to get laid. Can I help out?" he asked. "We could make it a threesome."

Tophet winced and bit back the vomit. "Stick to your own kind, mortal."

"I was just trying to help," he said, sounding put out.

She sat up. "Yeah, yeah. Look, you ruined the mood. I may as well get back to work." She sighed and as soon as she got to her feet, the couch disappeared.

Blaze patted Heather's bottom and said, "Maybe you and I could screw around some more?"

Heather giggled and reached out to tickle Blaze's waist. He flinched, laughed, then reached for her, but before they could get into a full-fledged tickle fight, Tophet stepped between them.

"Give me a break, will you? Coffee, Mortal Number Two. Now."

Heather hobbled to the coffee bar and made another pot. "You don't seem to be having much fun. It looks like burnout to me. Do you need a vacation?"

Tophet snorted. "Only desperately. I'd even settle for one day, one stupid holiday." She threw her hands in the air and went back to her cauldron.

"You have no vacation or holiday time?" Heather exclaimed. "After all these centuries of working you should have accrued a couple of years at least. Won't they give you a measly day off for something special?

"Nope. Nothing to celebrate and no one to celebrate with. Just the same old thing. Day after day. Day after day. Over and over again. I can't even get a few good hours of decent sleep and dream my way out of here. Someone has to distribute these souls. There's no end to the masochistic shlubs ready to go back and try living again." She heaved a huge sigh.

"Coffee," Heather announced, handing her the cup.

"What if no one tossed the souls for a while?" Blaze asked.

Tophet's eyes grew huge. "What if no one did this vitally important job? Are you mad?"

"No. I'm asking a perfectly legitimate question." He folded his arms and tried again. "What if you just said, 'To hell with it; I'm on strike. I'm going on vacation, and no one can stop me.'?"

She cocked her head to one side and thought about what he had said. "Actually, I don't know what would happen. I guess there would be less people born under the sign of Pisces." She thought long and hard about it as she drank her espresso.

Now that the scenario was firmly planted in her mind, she couldn't stop examining the possibilities. Walking away from the cauldron, Tophet scratched her platinum head and paced. "What would happen if I did say 'To hell with it'—which I never would since hell doesn't exist in several cultures—go on vacation, leaving no one in charge, and let all of my work go undone?" She shivered in horror as she pictured herself up to her hips in green ooze.

A long, steady stream of rocks fell into the pond.

"Oh, wet dog smell!" she cried.

"Hey, I know what we could do," Blaze said. "What if we offered to make and distribute the souls for you?"

Tophet squeezed her eyes shut. "Don't torture me! Here you are, willing to help, yet you're totally useless! The thought of it makes me long for that perfect expletive—soon. Oh, I wish I could take a vacation."

"Well, I guess there's no use wishing for what you can't have, is there?"

Tophet jammed her hands on her hips and yelled, "I'll wish all I want, boyo. I wish I could get away. I wish there was someone to fill-in for me. I wish I could find a tall, dark, and handsome immortal, preferably one who doesn't bite."

Heather sighed. "If you'll show us what to do, we could give it a try."

Tophet laughed. "You couldn't possibly..."

Another stream of rocks fell from the sky and pummeled the pond. She gritted her teeth. *I can't take much more of this.* "You know something, Mortal? I just might take you up on your suggestion. It used to be a lot of fun and I bet you'd do a good job. For you, it'll be fresh and new. You'll probably enjoy it so much you'll want to do it for years."

"Oh no!" Heather shrieked. "We are not staying for years. You were going to find us a way back, remember?"

"That's right. I said I would and I'm an immortal of my word." Tophet looked at the sky and sighed. An idea flashed through her mind, and she shouted, "Ah ha! I know what I can do to solve the problem." She clapped her hands and rubbed them together. "There's someone I need to see."

Heather jumped up and down. "That's great!"

Tophet pointed to Blaze. "You do the throwing. And you, Miss Sunshine, will decide where he should send the souls."

"You mean I get to be the one to make the decisions?" She stood straight and proud. "Just tell me what to do. I'm ready."

"I used to pitch in little league," Blaze offered.

Heather grinned with excitement. "We can do this and then you can find us a way out of here. Before you know it, you'll be on vacation! Oh, but you can't be gone for too long."

"It doesn't matter. I may be able to figure out a way to stop the blob downpour if I have a few minutes to think and another immortal to brainstorm with me, then the vacation would be short. Time passes very differently here, you know."

Tophet smiled and actually felt excited about something for the first time in eons. "Okay kids, you've watched me do it. Now what do you think you need to do first?"

"Well, I just take the spoon," Heather said. "Dip it into the pot and come out with a soul."

"Very good, Mortal Number Two. Then what?"

"Then I think of where I want the soul to be born and throw it as hard as I can."

"That's it!" Tophet tossed the metal spoon to her as if it were made of plastic.

Heather caught it with an 'Oomph!'. "Yikes, that's heavy."

While she was distracted, Blaze made a sneak attack on Heather's bottom, giving her a wedgie and a good spank.

"Good God, Heather! Why didn't I notice that gorgeous ass before?"

Heather jumped and giggled.

Tophet rolled her eyes. "Stop it, you two. You have to concentrate. It's not just grab and throw, but it's pretty simple if you can keep your mind on what you're doing. Give it a try Mortal Number One."

Blaze retrieved the spoon from Heather, fished out a soul and threw a fastball into the sky. They all watched with rapt attention as it disappeared.

"Perfect, Mortal Number One! Where did you send it?"

"Uh...I don't know."

Tophet dropped her forehead into her hands and said, "Oh no." She took a deep breath, yanked the spoon away from Blaze and offered it to Heather. "Here. Let's see what you can do, Mortal Number Two."

Heather dipped the spoon into the vat, pulled out a soul and spoke to it. "You are going to be born into a kind, loving family and grow up to be a responsible citizen." She tossed a wimpy underhand into the air. It fell back to earth with a plop. Tophet gasped, horrified. Heather handed her the spoon and muttered, "Darn."

"Um...don't worry, Mortal Number Two. It'll work out. I'm sure that with both of you working together, it can be done quite nicely." Tophet reversed her love spell and disappeared with a poof before either of them could change their minds.

CHAPTER SEVEN

Reappearing beside a shimmering, aquamarine swimming pool wearing a flowered sundress, Tophet plopped into an empty lounge chair. Her eyes swept over the posh resort, and she nodded her approval. She would have been completely happy if she didn't have to combine business with pleasure.

A drop-dead gorgeous, well-muscled man, who filled out his Speedo nicely, sat in the lounge chair next to her. She turned toward him and lowered her sunglasses.

Without glancing at her he spoke. "I hear you're looking for me."

Tophet sat bolt upright. "Death? Is that you?"

"In the flesh, so to speak." He reached over and proffered his hand.

She took it in hers and was shocked by its warmth. "My word, you've changed!"

He chuckled. "You haven't. Still looking for your perfect neologism, I take it?"

Tophet rolled her eyes. "Among other things. I've had some minor success with that. Listen to this. 'May your coleslaw be made of skunk cabbage!'

He raised his eyebrows.

"Oh, I didn't mean you, Death." She scanned him from top of his tousled black hair to his long toes. "You look hot! What happened?"

"You like it, Toffee baby? You can have all of me if you say the word."

She huffed. There was business to get out of the way first. "Tell me something. Why are you tossing me more souls than ever before, and in such large numbers each time?"

He smiled and flexed his left bicep, then his right. "I replicated myself and found the spare time to enjoy things again, like working out and swimming. It's made a world of difference."

She glanced at his studly body and felt the heat of desire begin to pool between her thighs. "I'll say. So, you cloned yourself, huh?"

"Yup. We split the duties. He does all the crappy, boring, individual jobs, and I take all the exciting disasters. Then I toss both of our collections your way at the same time."

She dropped his hand and jammed hers on her hips. "Well, that explains a few things."

Leaning back, he stretched languorously, placed his folded hands behind his head and displayed his magnificent body to its best advantage. Tophet couldn't help noticing he had grown a respectable amount of chest hair and powerful triceps. She swallowed a sigh.

A waitress walked over to them, a welcome diversion from the vision of gorgeousness lounging in the chair next to her. "Can I get you two anything?"

"Yes, please," Tophet said. "I'll have a Brandy Sling and my friend here will have a Bloody Mary."

"Certainly. Anything else?"

Tophet cocked her head to one side and studied the waitress for a moment. "Just answer one question for me. Do you like your job?"

"It's okay. Why do you ask?"

"Just curious."

As the waitress left to fill their order, Tophet mumbled under her breath, "Because with the two of us on vacation, you may be doing it for a long time."

Death laughed in his usual evil way. "You always did amuse me, Tophet. Especially recently. You got mortals to do your job for you. That's priceless. You know they can't sling souls for shit and yet you still let the stooges take over."

"I was in a bind. And by the way, how did you know about the mortals?"

He turned to her and grinned, then gazed deep into her eyes. "I've been keeping tabs on you."

"Be still my heart. So, poodle balls, you knew you were driving me crazy with the maddeningly heavy loads, I assume. The moments of frenzy followed by long stretches of boredom... Why did you keep doing it?"

"Humph, you obviously don't remember much about me." Death shrugged. "Because, my little frustrated one, I was hoping you'd join me in the lulls." He sat up and took her hand again. This time he enveloped it with the other one and stared into her eyes. "We'll both have to go back to work eventually or we'll have widespread longevity and a putrid pond of stagnant souls, but in the meantime..."

The waitress returned with their drinks, interrupting his thought.

"By the way," he said as he released her hand. "It was nice of you to remember my poison. What else do you remember about me?"

"Not much," she said.

He raised his eyebrows then shook his head.

The waitress patiently stood there.

"Put this on my tab, all right?"

The girl nodded and left. "I meant to say, I don't remember much of what I see in front of me right now. You've done some incredible self-improvements."

He sipped his Bloody Mary. "Yeah. I love that about me."

"I see your modesty has remained the same."

Death flashed his charming grin. "So, what did you come to see me about, Toffee baby?"

Tophet gritted her teeth. She was never quite sure how to take Death's favorite endearment, but she'd be damned if she'd let him know it bothered her. *If* it bothered her. She sort-of liked it but it made her feel less adult. He was only another immortal doing the other half of the same job. Their status was equal and yet he insisted on patronizing her, trying to act like her superior. *Maddening.*

"Okay. Now that I have you here, I'd like to discuss the criteria for transcending souls." She crossed her legs and wagged the top one. "It appears none of them are getting past me anymore. You can't tell me that Nirvana is full."

"Ha! That many perfect people transcending? Don't make me laugh."

"So, what's happening?"

"Didn't you get the memo?"

Tophet's brows knitted, and her leg stopped wagging. "Memo? What memo?"

Death moved to her lounge chair and sat beside her. He put an arm around her shoulder and took a deep breath. "There's no more transcending. Sorry, babe. They're all coming back to you, now."

"What?" She shrugged off his arm. "How the dangling, furry dice did that happen?"

"The great teachers, leaders and prophets aren't getting through to enough people to make a difference anymore. Until the mortals start listening to each other and working out their little problems on their own, they're all doomed to start over."

"You're... You've got to be..." Tophet threw an arm across her eyes and disappeared in a poof. She returned a moment later, dabbing her eyes with a tissue.

"Did you have a good cry?"

Tophet nodded. The lump in her throat didn't allow her to speak.

Death rubbed her back sympathetically. "I know, I know. I feel the same way. I used to be excited about my job. I even found it challenging. I used to have to think about where each soul needed to be. With you or with them? Now it's the same old thing. You, you, you, you, you..." He placed a finger under her chin and turned her face toward his. "Now all I can think about is you." He tipped his head to one side and focused on her lips, slowly leaning toward her.

She jerked back and frowned. "Not so fast, pal. If you want what I have, you need to prove yourself."

"Prove myself? Isn't my hot bod enough for you?"

"If you'll help me get rid of the mortals, you might look forward to me caressing that hot bod of yours."

"I need more than a caress and a maybe," he said.

"Okay, I'll get you off. Is it a deal?"

"Not yet. I want more than a little hand job. You've been holding me at bay for centuries."

In absolute frustration, Tophet threw her hands in the air and yelled, "So, what the fuck do you want?"

Death's white teeth gleamed. "That's it, Toffee baby. Exactly."

A pregnant woman in a maternity bathing suit was walking past them. Tophet barely noticed her until the woman jumped and screamed. Temporarily distracted, she looked up to see what made the woman yell and drop her lime Slurpee. Uh oh. It wasn't crushed ice on the cement walk. She saw neon-green Jell-O dripping off the woman's belly.

A huge sigh of disappointment escaped from deep in Tophet's diaphragm and her shoulders drooped. "I'd better get back to work. We'll finish discussing this later."

Death nodded and escorted a discouraged Tophet across the patio to a private spot. "I'll start working on your problem now, if you'll just say the word."

"What word?"

"I want you to say what you're going to do for me, if I help you."

Tophet shook her head. "I should never have left the pond."

"Say it."

"All right. I'll let you fuck me."

He chuckled. "And you won't just lie there either. Those are the terms."

Tophet threw her hands in the air. "It's just so routine. I thought a monkey could do it."

"I don't want a monkey, I want you."

Rolling her eyes, she said, "I meant slinging souls. You have a one-track mind."

"So when will I see you again?"

"I came to you this time. It's your turn to come to me."

Death waved his hand. In a flash he was clothed in his traditional black robe, holding his scythe. "If you need me, call."

"Sure. I'll do that." She poofed her way back to the pond, secretly delighted with the business meeting.

CHAPTER EIGHT

Tophet walked up to Heather from behind. "Give me that ladle before you hurt yourself." As soon as Tophet appropriated it, she spotted green gel all over the grass. "Oh, moldy moth balls! What did you do?"

"What do you mean?" Heather looked surprised. "We did all right, didn't we? I found very nice families for all of those good souls and Blaze threw them, just like you instructed."

"Yeah, nice families with green goop splattered all over them from outer space."

Heather set her hands on her hips. "We did the best we could."

"You're right." Tophet crossed her arms. "You did a commendable job—for a couple of nincompoop mortals. I guess I expected too much."

"Well, we tried." Blaze stooped over and tried to pick up the goo he had dropped in the grass. Most of it slipped through his fingers, but he was able to scrape up part of the mess with his hands.

"Did you find out how to get us home?" Heather asked.

"Not yet."

Tophet couldn't help but snicker as she watched the wet, runny substance slip through Blaze's fingers and drip right back onto the ground.

He stood up straight and glared at her. "Hey, that was rotten what you did to us. You barely trained us, went off and had your vacation and didn't even find a solution to our problem."

Heather frowned and nodded. "Yeah, what he said. And you shouldn't laugh at him."

Tophet put her hand over her grin and tried to look serious. "I know, but you shouldn't worry about Mortal Number One's feelings so much. After all, you think he's a little light on the brain cells, right?"

"I do not!"

Oh good, my evil plan's still working. But just to be sure... "I can make him smarter." Tophet aimed her spoon.

"Leave him alone. I love him just the way he is." Heather went to wipe her gloppy hands on her dress but thought better of it. Instead, she wiped them on the grass next to Blaze, kissing him on the cheek when she was done.

Tophet smirked. "Aww, come on. Let me make him smarter."

Heather grabbed Blaze's arm and said, "No, don't change a hair on his head."

"Okay." No sooner had Tophet agreed, than she pointed the spoon at Blaze, and he jumped as if zapped with an electric shock.

Blaze's eyes widened. "E equals MC squared and damn, I even understand that."

"I told you not to change him," Heather cried.

"You told me not to change a hair on his head. A few brain cells inside are rewired now, but the hair on his head is exactly as it was."

Blaze rolled his eyes. "So how did that vacation go? Did you find your friend? Did you get anywhere at all?"

Tophet sighed. "Yes. I had to compromise my principles for help in getting you back home and there are still no guarantees. Sad, really. I would have enjoyed bumping uglies with him if he hadn't used it as a bribe."

Heather stiffened and tilted her head. "What? Who?"

"You'll see."

"You said you were all alone."

"No, I didn't."

Blaze put his arm around Heather. "In other words, what you're saying is you offered to sleep with someone in exchange for getting us out of here?"

Heather gasped and slapped a hand over her mouth.

Tophet's lounge chair materialized, and she stretched out seductively on it. "It's no big deal, Mortal Number Two. I'd have done worse."

"What's worse than prostituting yourself?"

Tophet snickered. "Truth be told, prostituting myself to that particular immortal isn't much of a sacrifice at all. I'm no idiot."

Blaze crossed his arms. "So, what happened to those souls we tossed that didn't make it to their destinations?"

After a deep sigh, she admitted, "I don't know. There's never been a precedent."

Heather gave up trying to be polite and wagged a finger at her. "I think all of us have something to think about—including you, Tophet. You should be ashamed of yourself."

"For what? For trying to help you, little Miss Ingrate?"

"No. I don't care who you sell your body to, but what about what you did to the two of us, and who knows how many others! You should've stayed long enough to make sure we were doing the job right, that we were helping. I shudder to think what we've done to those poor souls. I feel terrible knowing we may have hurt them. You should feel bad too."

"Yeah, we thought we were helping, but instead we're going to have to live with the knowledge that we may have really screwed up," Blaze chimed in.

Tophet stood up. Her lounge once again disappeared. "Yeah, well, I'm here now." She reached for and grabbed the spoon. "Go fetch me another cup of coffee, will you?"

Heather didn't move.

Tophet was sure they'd probably forget all about it and go back to fornicating in the bushes again before long, but there was something else on Mortal Number Two's mind.

"So…You think I should make it up to you somehow?"

"Jeez. I keep forgetting you can read our minds. That's freaky." Heather wiped the last of the goop from her hands onto the grass and said, "Yeah. I think you should."

"Okay. I don't know how wise this is, but I know you've been dying to ask me about your past lives. Would a little peek into one or two of them satisfy you?"

"I'd love that."

Blaze perked up. "I would too."

Tophet rubbed her hands together. *This should be fun.* "First of all, what do you know about reincarnation?"

Blaze scratched his chin and thought out loud. "Well, I've heard things, but I don't really *know* anything for sure."

A leather armchair appeared, and Tophet made herself comfortable. "What have you heard?"

"One thing I've heard is if you're having trouble with someone in this life, then they may have been in your past life too.

If you don't work things out before you die, you have to go through it again and again until you make things right."

"That's partly true. You do come back with some of the same people. If people can discern what went wrong between them in a past life, it should provide an insight into why things are going wrong in their present life. However, it never happens. The good news is that just by making peace, you can still transcend the trouble and avoid it next time."

"Oh. That's good to know," Heather said.

"You're thinking, of course, about the trouble you're having with your mother."

Heather nodded.

Tophet conjured a matching love seat and motioned for her to sit. "This might be hard to swallow but here's what happened. Your mother used to be your sister. There's sibling rivalry left over but it's stronger than usual. You see, you were a beautiful woman, your sister was an ugly cow. She resented your success as well as your beauty, since your earnings as a prostitute supported the whole family. Your sister couldn't get laid for free and was sent off to be a slave."

"I was a what?"

"A prostitute. Streetwalker. Lady of the evening. Didn't you hear me? I'm sitting right beside you."

Heather wrung her hands and rested them in her lap. "There's no chance you could be wrong about that?"

Tophet spoke with authority. "Nope. No chance whatsoever."

Blaze sat on the grass in front of them and said, "I don't know, Heather...I think that's kinda hot."

She smiled and batted her eyelashes at him before turning back to look at Tophet. "So why did you make her my mother this time?"

"I thought I'd give her the upper hand in this lifetime to balance the two of you out. Does that answer your question?"

Heather sighed. "I guess so, but why is she so determined to get me to enter beauty pageants, if that's the case?"

"Simple. So, she can watch you fail."

Heather gasped. "That's awful! She'd never do that. She loves me. You take that back."

"Hey, I didn't know she was going to do that. Maybe next time I'll make her a chimpanzee."

Heather stared at Tophet wide-eyed. "No way. Isn't there something else we can do to stop this cycle?"

"Just forgive her. That'll work as long as it's genuine."

Heather blew out a deep breath and looked at her feet. "I'll try."

"Can you tell me if I ever had a good life?" Blaze asked. "Was I famous or anything?"

Tophet stood and clasped her hands behind her back. "Sure. You were an Olympic athlete in ancient Greece."

"I was?"

"Yes. You threw the Javelin and you were great. Almost unbeatable."

He smiled. "Really?"

"Really." Tophet jammed her hands on her hips and leaned toward Blaze until his smile faded. "That's why I was deluded into thinking you could throw something and hit a target!"

"We said we were sorry!"

"Yes, you did." The cauldron began to bubble, so Tophet picked up the spoon and gave it a stir. "And I forgave you. You're energetic and you like to try new things, but you can grovel when you fail. I like that about the two of you."

"I'm not groveling," he said. "It was your fault anyway. If you had fucking trained us..."

"Yes, yes. I understand. Tell you what...you decide what kind of life you want to go back to next time and maybe I'll hit the target."

"Thanks a pant-load," Blaze muttered.

"You can be sent backwards you know!" Tophet stopped stirring and saw Blaze turn white. "Nah, I'm just kidding. That's like a parent threatening to return their child to the stork."

She resumed stirring the bubbling substance. "I'd better get these souls blended. If they sit too long they start to harden, and then I'll be sending criminals into the world. Not that there aren't plenty of dysfunctional families to abuse and neglect them..."

Several more rocks dropped into the pond and Tophet shook her fist at the sky. "Dog balls!" She let out a deep sigh. "Hey! That felt good."

While stirring, Tophet asked, "So, Mortal Number One, do I still deserve a good spanking for what I did?"

"Don't try to cheer me up."

"Fine, I won't. I need to get caught up anyway. I'm as busy as a postal worker at Christmas and only a little less disgruntled." She pulled out a spoonful of green goo, checked it quickly and then tossed it overhand into the sky above the tree line.

"Is there a way to speed things up?" Blaze asked.

Tophet sneered. "I've been doing it this way for eons. What makes you think there's a better way?"

Heather scratched her head. "Sometimes when I'm at work and trying to catch up, I look at the things I'm doing and ask myself why it's being done that way. If the answer is 'because it's always been done that way', I try to think of better, smarter, more efficient methods."

"So, Mortals, since you're questioning my efficiency, I'm interested to hear what your suggestions are for improving my methods."

"I—I can't think of anything right now," Heather said.

Blaze picked a blade of grass and examined it. "We'll think about it when we get back home—if we get back." He slanted an accusatory look at Tophet. "What did you find out while you were off, leaving us, untrained, to pick up your slack?"

"No need to be so rude, Moral Number One." *Or I'll make you wish you had been born during the Bubonic plague next time.*

She handed him the long metal spoon. "Here's your opportunity to improve my efficiency. Simply point and shoot."

"Excuse me?"

Tophet rolled her eyes. "Jeez. Haven't you learned anything? Aim it at whatever you want and project your thoughts."

Blaze swept the spoon over the pond and pointed it at the grass. A child-sized wading pool appeared, half-filled with the green glop of souls. He then pointed the spoon toward the woods and two nymphs in bikinis ran out from behind the trees. They jumped into the plastic pool and began stomping on the souls as if they were grapes.

"No, no, no!" Tophet cried. "Gently, you fools."

Blaze pointed the spoon at the nymphs. They lay down and rolled around in the goo. As soon as they were completely covered and green, they commenced combat as if mud wrestling but instead of mud it was gloppy green souls.

Tophet shook her head and walked away. "You have a warped mind Mortal Number One, but your idea is so crazy it just might work."

Blaze crossed his arms and looked as smug as Death.

"Okay. So, you had one decent idea. Don't get cocky."

Tophet glanced over at the nymphs and said to Blaze, "Gives wrestling with your soul a whole new meaning, doesn't it?"

She crooked her finger at the young couple. "Come here Number One and Number Two. I want to show you something." Tophet led the way to the edge of the pond. She reached out her hand for the spoon. "Give me that."

Leaning as far over the pond as she could, she pulled up one of the hard, withered rocks that resembled a prune. Then she gathered a nice spoonful of green gelatin closer to the shore, and handed Blaze the two souls, placing one in each hand. "Can you tell the difference?"

He balanced them in his hands, as if comparing weights and then smelled them. Just as he stuck out his tongue, prepared to taste the gelatinous one, Tophet interrupted.

"Oh, snake slime! Of course, you can tell the difference! One's a used up old turd of a soul and the other is completely regenerated."

She took both of the souls in her hands and held up the dark, wrinkled one. "To recycle this"—then she held up her other hand—"into *this* is fairly simple. Actually, I do nothing. All I can do is wait. As far as I know there's no way to speed that up. If you think of something..." She dropped both souls back into the pond and gazed at the gel-covered nymphs. "Tell me about it first, will you?"

Wandering over to the wrestling pit, she held up one hand. The bikini-clad girls stopped what they were doing and stood, dripping green, glowing liquid.

"Let me check the consistency." No sooner had Tophet leaned over the small plastic pool than the two nymphs pulled her face-first into the souls, jumped out and ran for the woods, giggling.

Almost immediately she surfaced, shaking her slimy, green fist at them. "You'd better run. I can turn you into Mormons and make you join *Up with People*."

Tophet stepped out of the pool, every bit of gel remaining behind as if she had walked through a car wash.

"Well, let's assess the damage." She pulled two handfuls of wiggly but cohesive gel out of the pool and smiled. "Look at these two. Soul mates. Who says I'm not sentimental?" She moved her hands closer together. "Lifetime after lifetime, they find each other and fall in love all over again."

Heather sighed. "That's so beautiful."

Tophet pitched one as hard as she could to the east and the other just as hard to the west. Then she snickered and slapped her own face. "Oh, I'm so bad."

"What did you just do?" Heather cried.

"Oh relax. They'll find each other. It'll just take a little more effort this time, that's all."

With a smug look on her face, Tophet strutted around Blaze and Heather. "Now let's imagine the two of you were soul mates. Stepping into that elevator wouldn't have been an accident."

Blaze wrinkled his brow. "You're kidding."

"Oh, I don't think so."

"Really? We're soul mates?" Heather exclaimed. "And to think, we get to know it's forever right away. I mean, is it... Do we...?"

"Oh yes. There's a long white dress in your future, Mortal Number Two."

"Oh, thank you!"

"Don't mention it. And Mortal Number One is gonna look terrific in his leather tux."

"Cool! I didn't know they made 'em, but I can't wait to try one on." He picked up Heather and swung her around.

Tophet began to return to the cauldron when she stopped, teetered, and moaned. Her chaise appeared underneath her as she dropped her body onto it.

Caressing her breasts, she moaned louder. "Oh… Oh…"

"She's doing it again," Blaze said.

Heather looked embarrassed. "I think she must have been reading my mind. I—I was just thinking about our honeymoon."

"I'd like to do it sooner than the honeymoon. Maybe right now since she's preoccupied. Besides, I think we'd better give her some privacy. Would you like to take a walk around the pond with me?"

Heather grinned. "Sure."

Tophet stopped and looked at them. "Wait…voyeurism can be fun, and exhibitionism can make you really hot for each other." She began to arch her back, shudder and moan louder, to demonstrate her point.

"Sorry. I think we're plenty hot. We'll be on our way now," Blaze said. He placed his hand gently on Heather's back, escorting her to the path around the pond. "Have fun," he called over his shoulder. "I know we will." Blaze smiled and patted Heather's ass.

Once the two lovebirds were far enough away to effectively hide in the tall reeds and grass on the opposite side of the pond, Blaze stopped and spun Heather to face him. He dropped down on one knee and Heather's hands flew to cover her open mouth.

"Heather, will you do me the honor of marrying me even though I'm a piss-poor excuse for a provider? At least you know I'm a damn good lover and I promise I'll fuck you silly at every reasonable opportunity."

"Oh yes!" she squealed.

As she dove into his waiting arms, she accidentally tackled him to the ground and the two of them rolled in the grass, laughing.

"Heather, I love you. You're exactly what I want in a woman. I'm going to make you come without even undressing you."

"I think I just did."

CHAPTER TEN

"Hello?"

Tophet ignored the voice and tried to get back to work.

"Hello?" The female voice persisted. "Hello?"

"Oh myself!" Tophet yelled.

The sexy female voice called out to her again. "Hello?"

Tophet glared at the sky. "Oh, cross-eyed frogs! It's someone going through one of those past life regressions again."

"Goddess, can you show me my soul mate?"

"Why yes, I can. But you may be a bit surprised," she scoffed.

"I'm prepared. Show him to me so I can recognize him."

"That may be a challenge, but if you really want this..."

"I do. I do," crooned the sexy female voice.

Tophet turned the spoon around and waved the handle at the sky. A visual representation of a pregnant woman by a community pool was conjured."

"Oh my God!"

"What?" She shrugged. "He's a nice kid. Of course, he used to be Billy the Kid, but none of that will matter to you when you start babysitting him."

"Ick!" The intruding female presence disappeared, and Tophet shook her head. "I hate past life regressions! Why is everyone constantly interrupting my work with stupid questions?"

Tophet returned to work and pitched a few more souls when Heather and Blaze emerged from the other side of the pond, holding hands.

When she saw them whispering to each other, giggling, seeming content and happy. Tophet continued to spout off to no one in particular. "Who's my soul mate?" She sing-songed. "Show him to me so I can recognize him... Dog balls. Dog balls!"

She swung her spoon back and forth and then pointed it at Blaze and Heather. They reared back and shielded themselves, but nothing happened.

"Let me explain something," she snarled. "Soul mates recognize each other on a nonphysical level. That explains some of the weirdest couples—you two, for instance."

"Don't make fun of us," Heather said.

"I thought you wanted me to have fun!" Tophet roared.

Jumping in apparent fright, Heather dropped her crutches and fell on her butt again.

"Nice going, Tophet." Blaze picked up Heather's crutches and helped her to her feet. "If she falls again and breaks her other leg, she'll never be able to compete in the Miss Georgia pageant."

Tophet chuckled. "She still intends to do that, does she? Doesn't that strike you as a lot of foolishness?"

Blaze smiled at Heather and kissed her palm. "Not if that's what she wants."

Tophet rolled her eyes when she heard Heather's sigh, and stuck her finger down her throat, pretending to make herself gag. "Why the dog balls did I ask a mortal soul mate a question like that, knowing I'd get a moronic answer?"

At that moment a golden retriever raced across the lawn and headed straight for the pond. Horrified, Tophet ran after the dog, shouting at it. "Get out of there you mangy mutt! Shoo! Go 'way!"

The dog had begun lapping the water when a young woman rushed to the dog's side and grabbed him. She looped a collar around his neck and pulled him away by his leash.

"I'm so sorry. I have no idea how that happened. I've never had an animal get loose from the pound of souls before." She turned to the dog and wagged her finger at him. "Bad Balls. You're a very bad dog, Balls. You have your own drinking water. Now, back to the pound!"

As she led him away, Tophet covered her mouth with her hands. A muffled scream of frustration escaped through her fingers. She dropped her hands and inhaled deeply, trying to regain control. "That's just freakin' great. Now I have to come up with *another* expression."

When she heard snickering coming from behind her, she turned around to glare at them.

Blaze draped his arm over Heather's shoulder. "You've got to admit, that was pretty funny. Was that another immortal we just saw?"

"No. That must have been another fill-in. That never would have happened if the animals were being cared for properly."

"So how many immortals are there?" Heather asked.

"I don't really know." Tophet scratched her head. "I only deal with certain ones. I imagine there are others, but I'm on a need-to-know basis."

Heather looked up at her with wide, blue eyes. "Do you know God?"

"God?" Tophet rubbed her neck and puzzled over the question, frowning. "I guess you mean the big guys?"

Heather's eyes grew ever larger. "Guys?"

"That's just an expression. It doesn't mean men. There are two equal entities, and for lack of a better explanation, one is female and the other male. It's a balance of power necessary to make decisions affecting the world, the universe, the dimensions... It's like the system of checks and balances in democracy."

Blaze cocked his head to one side. "Is that why nothing ever gets done?"

"Um...it's complicated. I'll try to explain it to you before you leave, but if you don't stop distracting me, you never will! How about another cup of espresso?"

Tophet paced and pouted until Heather returned with her steaming hot coffee. She took a sip and sighed. "I wish I could find another immortal to babysit. I only know two that I could ask, and well...neither one is a good idea."

"Isn't there a nice immortal?" Heather asked.

"Well, yes, there was..."

Heather sucked in a deep breath and slapped a hand over her heart. "Was? What happened?"

"Oh—nothing. Not really." Tophet paced faster and shrugged a lot. "She's, um...tied up. I mean, she's just very busy. Taking care of the moon and stuff."

Heather crossed her arms and looked at the mysterious one with suspicion. "Something sounds fishy here. What are you trying to hide?"

"Okay. Okay, fine. I don't really know where she is, I kind of forget where we..." Tophet shrugged again.

Blaze looked at her askance. "Where you what?"

Tophet stopped pacing, blew out a long breath and looked at the sky. "Okay. You asked for it." She called out in a long, reverberating echo, "Death... Oh Death..."

The ground shook. The mortals trembled and held onto one another. In a flash of lightning, Death made his grand entrance in all of his black-caped and hooded glory. Tophet's two frightened guests screamed.

"Now that's not a very nice greeting," he said, leaning on his scythe. "How do you think that makes me feel?"

They huddled closer together.

"You've obviously been given the wrong impression of me. I'm not scary; I'm cool."

"B-but, you wear a black robe and hood, and you k-kill people!" Blaze stuttered.

Death hummed the same kind of eerie tune they had first heard from Tophet, then he began singing his own song.

I wore black before black was cool.
Hidden from view, I'm nobody's fool.
Is that why everybody fears me?

I'm intimidating, that's for sure.
When I say 'Come', you don't wonder what for.
Is that why everybody fears me, baby?

I'm not a bad guy,
I just have a bad job,
but somebody has to do it.
I thought I would try
to let a few by,
but I knew by the Gods

I blew it.

So I wear black in the shape of a sack
And now there is no looking back.
Is that why everybody fears me, baby?

In mourning clothes, the reaper knows
everyone comes and everyone goes,
so why does everybody fear me, baby?

Tophet crossed her arms and rolled her eyes. "Death, where's the Moon Goddess? The one we—um, well...you know..."

"Why do you care?"

She indicated the mortals with her thumb and spoke softly. "They're asking questions."

He laughed and patted Tophet on the head. "Oh, she's okay. She's on the other side of the rainbow. Don't you remember, Darling? You said, 'This is my pond, and you can go—'"

"Shh!"

Death straightened his spine and gave Tophet an intense stare. "I hate being shushed. What's up with you?"

Tophet ignored his remark and crossed her arms. "Just get her back."

He pointed to the mortals with his scythe. "Why? Are they from Amnesty Interdimensional?"

"No..." She lowered her voice to a whisper. "It's been a while since we checked on her. I think we'd better."

Death nodded. "Let me go first and check it out. The last time you checked on her, you came back a little worse for wear, if I remember correctly." He disappeared and reappeared behind her in almost simultaneous bursts.

Tophet whirled around and gawked at him. "That's it? Poof, poof?"

"That's the secret, babe. Get in. Get out."

"So, what do you think? Is it safe to send the mortals over to her for a while?"

He burst into hardy laughter. "She's a Crone now. There's no danger there."

"A Crone?" Her eyes widened as she pondered the possible meaning of this. "An old woman? But how?"

"Moon phases, babe. Isn't injustice wonderful?"

She clasped her hands behind her back and paced back and forth, trying to come to terms with that particular bit of news. "So, is she mellow now?"

"She was until she saw me. Apparently, her memory is still intact."

"But will the mortals be safe?" She halted a few feet from the anxious pair in question.

Death slid up beside her and murmured in her ear. "Do we care?"

Tophet smiled, swooped her arms in the direction of the sky and said, "Off they go."

CHAPTER ELEVEN

Blaze and Heather disappeared in one large, lightning-flash poof. When the smoke cleared, Death was stroking Tophet's back. His hand ran lightly over her long hair and stopped to cup her ass.

"So...it's just you and me, alone at last."

"Don't be cocky. You haven't helped much, yet."

With one swift step he faced her and rubbed his long, hard ridge over her abdomen. "I can't help that. See what you do to me?"

She chuckled but didn't try to move away.

Death ground his hard-on into her pelvis. "I'd love to pick up where we left off before you and old Moon-eyes got into your jealous rages over me."

"Oh, give me a break. It had nothing to do with you."

"Oh yeah? What was it then?" He licked the rim of her ear before slipping his tongue inside.

She shivered as she remembered his talented tongue. Maybe it has been too long since...

His warm breath replaced his tongue in her sensitive ear. "Ohh...

"C'mon, baby. Let's live a little."

"That's easy for you to say." She decided to let him think he had to work for it, especially since she loved being seduced, and he did seduction so well.

He reached for her breast, his fingers shaking, but before he could make contact, she swiveled her torso away.

Death stomped his foot. "What is it now? What did or didn't I do to deserve this tease?"

"It's nothing you did. It's what I want."

He crossed his arms and leveled his gaze at her, suspicion in his eyes. "What do you want?"

"Two things. I want you to help me with the mortals—either they get sent back or you'll be babysitting them for the next four years."

"What? You've got to be—"

"And, I want you to stop bombarding me with so many souls all at once."

Death tapped his foot and stared at her. She shimmied out of the remainder of her robe knowing her breasts and long legs would drive him to distraction. For good measure she stepped out of the robe crumpled around her ankles, turned around and bent over from her waist to pick it up. Then she laid it out on the ground like a picnic blanket, the whole time feeling his searing gaze on her bare ass.

"Oh, all right, all right! I'll do it."

She sat on the blanket, leaned back on her elbows, and spread her legs. "That'll depend on how long Moonbeam is willing to keep the mortals."

Death grabbed the top of his robe and tore it off over his head. He loomed above her, exposing his fabulous new body and his luscious, erect cock. "Then let's not waste any time," he demanded. "Talk dirty to me."

"I thought you wanted to get to the fucking?"

"Oh, I do." He stroked his cock and instantly grew hard. "Flip over for me, will ya?"

She frowned, rose, and jammed her hands on her hips. "Not yet. What about me?"

"Oh. Sure," he mumbled. "What would you like first?"

She thrust out her chest.

"My pleasure." He produced a bed with a wave of his hand and pulled her down next to him. She wiggled her ass and placed clasped hands behind her head, getting comfortable.

Death dove for her breasts. His suction resembled an industrial strength vacuum cleaner and Tophet groaned in pain as she pushed him off the bed. He landed on the ground with a thud.

"What was that for?"

"Gently, Mr. Enthusiastic. You almost Hoovered my tits down your throat."

Death grinned. "Sorry baby. Guess I got carried away."

"Getting carried away is fine, but try to leave me in one piece, okay?"

"It's just that it's been so long, Toffee. Why didn't you believe me when I said the Goddess and I were just friends?"

"Because you were lying."

"I wasn't! You've heard of friends with benefits, haven't you?"

Tophet rolled over and faced away from him.

Death heaved himself to his feet and walked around to the side she was facing. "It didn't mean anything, baby." She rolled to the other side.

He jogged around the bed to face her. "It was a mistake. One lousy mistake. I'll never make that mistake again. Come on, lover. Now that I know how you feel, I'm all yours."

Tophet lifted her head and glared at him. "Oh yeah? Tell me how I feel."

He slid into bed and reached for her. When she didn't respond but didn't shrink away, he settled for tracing patterns on her stomach. "You're hurt, but you're still crazy about me. I don't blame you, baby, but at the time we hadn't discussed anything about not seeing other immortals. I should have realized you loved me, but I—"

"Loved you?" She pushed herself up to a sitting position and laughed.

Death moved toward her and slipped an arm around her waist. "Well, you cared, didn't you? If you didn't care, it wouldn't have mattered who I fooled around with."

She lightly stroked the dark, shiny hair on his muscled arm. "I guess so."

"Okay then, are you ready to go or what?"

Tophet frowned at him. "That's it? That's all the foreplay I get? Oh, I'm ready to go all right." She was dressed and on the other side of the pond in a poof.

"Ah, peace and quiet at last." She lowered herself into a beach chair. "Now maybe I can think of a much-needed obscenity."

Death materialized next to her.

"Oh, hog mud!"

"I've never seen you like this, Toffee. What's going on?"

She leaned forward and shrugged. "I can't help it. I can't concentrate. I keep wondering if they're really all right with her...moody bitch."

Death looked at the sky and let out a deep breath. "Toffee, Toffee..."

"If you can help me find a way to get them back before midnight, I might be able to get back in the mood."

"Hold that thought. I can feel an accident about to happen." Death disappeared in a flash of lightening.

Tophet collapsed backward against the chair. "You're an accident waiting to happen." She struggled out of her chair and pondered their relationship with all its ramifications. Then thoughts of the mortals intruded. Throwing her hands in the air, she exclaimed, "I can't stand it! I have to bring them back."

Blaze appeared in a puff of smoke, but he was alone. No Heather.

"What the heck happened to Mortal Number Two?" she shouted.

Blaze glanced around. "I don't know. The last I saw; she was engrossed in a deep conversation with the Goddess."

"You let that witch fill her head full of lies and then left her there? How could you?"

Blaze shrugged. "I didn't have much choice in the matter, did I?"

A full five seconds later, Heather reappeared. Blaze put an arm around her and kissed her on the temple. "What kept you? I missed you, honey."

Tophet shook her finger at her. "Don't ever do that again, young lady! You had me worried sick. Where have you been?"

"But—"

"No buts! No excuses. I don't want to hear it. In fact, from now on just be quiet and listen. Don't speak unless spoken to! Understand?"

"Bu—"

"What did I just say? No talking! I'm so mad I'm not even going to read your mind anymore. Now get me more coffee."

Heather bit her lip, looked down at the ground and silently nodded.

"Now, Mortal Number One, did you have a good time with old Moon-face?"

"Yeah, she was okay. She had some pretty wild stories about you and Death, though." Blaze shook his head. "If we'd met her first, we'd have been petrified of you!"

Tophet crossed her arms, her long, flowing sleeves fluttering with the movement. "But you *were* petrified of me. And as far as I know, you're still petrified of Death. Most humans are."

Heather returned with the coffee and Tophet accepted it without giving her so much as a smile and continued to talk to Blaze. "Some welcome him, though. He can be quite charming and compassionate, if he's treated with the respect he deserves."

"Respect?" Blaze thought a moment. "Yeah, I guess so. He does kind of have the power of life and death over us."

Tophet rolled her eyes and produced two chairs across from each other. She sat facing Blaze. "You're talking about fear. Respecting Death isn't about power or fear. It's about recognizing his place in the natural order of things."

"That's not what I meant."

Frantically, Heather tapped him on the shoulder, and gestured at him by the motion of zipping her mouth.

Tophet produced another chair for Heather and said, "Sit. Both of you."

They did as they were told, but both balanced on the edge of their seats as if ready to jump up and run.

Tophet leveled her gaze at them. "Okay, what did the old wise-one tell you?"

Blaze inhaled deeply, appearing to gather his courage, and said, "She seemed to think you and Death ganged up on her and banished her to another place."

"Oh, that." She leaned back and made herself comfortable. "She provoked the whole thing, you know. I don't suppose she told you anything about her traitorous behavior, did she?"

When they both mutely shook their heads, she took a deep breath and launched into an explanation she thought they would understand. "Death and I were tight, you know? We had a good thing going on between us. No one should interfere with something like that, and she did."

"What did she do?"

"She was young, all-knowing and glowing, and she was trying to steal my guy!"

Heather opened her mouth to speak, her expression conveying her intentions to defend the Goddess, but Tophet pointed a finger at her face, her glare daring her to do something foolish. She hoped she looked like an old-west outlaw about to cut her down. She must have presented the right persona. Heather clammed up.

"Well, we didn't really believe all the things she said, anyway." Blaze scratched his head. "She did mention something about the whole non-transcending thing though, and I thought of a question I'd like to ask you."

Interested, Tophet cocked her head to one side. "Ask away, Mortal Number One."

"If we manage to get out of here, do we take some kind of knowledge back home? Like, what really happens to us after we die and what we need to do to start transcending again?"

Tophet fidgeted and looked off into the distance. Not wanting to admit she didn't know the answer, she blustered instead. "Interruptions! Always with the interruptions you two. No wonder I can't get any work done. I have a whole vat of ripe souls waiting for me, and if I don't get to them soon, we'll have another baby boom.

"Now why don't you two go and bother someone else for a while? Like Death! Go ask him for the transcending criteria. Maybe, if you keep him distracted for a while, I can catch up."

Tophet waved her arms and their eyes widened for a fraction of a second—then they were gone.

CHAPTER TWELVE

When the smoke cleared, Blaze and Heather found themselves in a roadside ditch about ten feet from a car wreck. Death stepped out of the vehicle, wearing rubber gloves dripping with blood. "Well, that was messy," he mumbled to himself.

He pulled a red bag from his robe and the bloody gloves vanished into the opaque, red plastic. It jiggled slightly before he tucked it away. He looked over toward them and jumped. "Whoa, how did you get here?"

"Tophet sent us," Blaze said.

"Well, don't sneak up on immortals like that. You nearly scared me to death." He chuckled at his own joke and wandered over to where they stood. "Remind me to thank her. To what do I owe the intrusion of your company?"

"We asked her a question and she said we should ask you."

"All right. You'll need to come along with me as I work, though. Promise you won't cry, vomit or faint." Death climbed out of the ditch, and they scrambled to follow him, glancing at each other anxiously.

"Okay, so what's your question?"

"What does it take to transcend to the next level?"

"You're kidding? She asked you to ask me? Boy, she must have been thoroughly sick of looking after you."

A flash and puff of smoke later, Death was wearing an argyle sweater and brown slacks, standing at a podium in front of a blackboard. Two folding chairs were empty in front of him and all of this in the middle of the road. He gestured to the chairs until the mortal 'students' sat.

"There's only one thing you need to accomplish, but it's very hard for humans to do apparently. Transcending can take several lifetimes, but it's so simple you'll kick yourselves for not thinking of it. Any guesses?"

They looked at each other and then looked at Death. Blaze shrugged and said, "Learning our lessons?"

Death folded his arms, his usual smug expression on his face, and asked, "What lessons?"

"I don't know. That's what I was asking you, I think."

Death shook his head and paced back and forth in front of the blackboard. "There's one thing you must overcome. Now think. What might that be?"

"Only one thing?"

"Yes; one thing. You get plenty of opportunities to practice overcoming it until you realize what it is, then you make avoiding it altogether a permanent part of your value and belief system. Once you embrace the simple truth—"

Heather raised her hand.

Death made a point of looking all around him, as if he didn't even see her until she was waving her hand madly. "Yes, Mortal Number Two?"

"May I go to the bathroom?"

"Class is almost over, can it wait a minute?"

She put her hand down. "I guess so."

Death shrugged. "No one has the answer? Well then, I'll tell you. Mortals need to overcome all of their tendencies toward destructivity."

Heather elbowed Blaze and whispered, "I don't think there's any such word as 'destructivity'."

"Excuse me Mortal Number Two, do you want to come up here and teach the class?"

She looked like she was about to say something until Death loomed large and lightning flashed, thunder following close behind. Her face leeched of color and she shook her head sheepishly.

Death resumed his former poise and casually said, "I didn't think so." The podium and blackboard disappeared and after a quick flash, Death reappeared in his flowing robe, holding his scythe.

He began to walk away, and the mortals followed him at a distance. Blaze turned around to see that although the chairs were gone, the car was still there. He saw a body slumped over the steering wheel and automatically held out his hand to a pale Heather. She clasped it tightly as if he were her only hold on to reality. They picked up their pace and soon entered a small town.

Without turning around, Death asked, "Did I frighten you?"

"Me? Sort of. Heather's plenty scared, though."

"Good, I haven't lost my touch then."

"Why do you hate us?"

Death stopped and turned halfway to look at them. "I don't hate you, but it's interesting how my little demonstration made you think I did. Pretty intimidating, wasn't I?"

Blaze scratched his head. "Yeah. Is that what you mean by destructivity?"

Death resumed walking, looking straight ahead, and raised his fluttering sleeves in an expansive gesture. "Molesting kids; senseless gang violence; humans taking other human lives for stupid or unscrupulous reasons. The stuff I have nothing to do with."

"What about accidents?"

"Accidents happen. That's not destructivity."

"What about bad attitudes? Cynicism or sarcasm?"

"No, that's what makes life bearable. Now wait here while I go choke someone, okay?"

They had stopped outside a restaurant. Blaze and Heather stood on the sidewalk while Death went inside.

Heather turned toward Blaze and whispered, "Is he going in there to kill somebody?"

"I—I guess so."

She buried her face in his soft, grey T-shirt and he pulled her close. "Heather, I don't know if this is such a good idea. Maybe we should go..."

Death reappeared, taking off his rubber gloves. "Now that was a classy death. Choked on Filet Mignon and never knocked over the Champagne glass."

"Uh, Death? We were wondering if we could just hitch a ride and go home now. We're in America, right?"

"Wrong. You're in another dimension. Do you see anyone reacting to us?"

Blaze looked around. People were walking by, getting into cars, just looking like they were going about a normal afternoon. No one even glanced their way.

"Can't they see us?" Blaze spotted a man walking right toward him.

"What do you think?"

He moved to where he knew the man would bump into him at any second, but instead of colliding with each other, he passed straight through him. Blaze felt a warm sensation where the man had been and when he whirled around, he noticed the man shiver and pull his jacket tighter.

"Hey, what the...? Are we ghosts?"

"Not in the dead sense of the word."

Death opened a purple, velvet pouch and shook out a few rocks. "I'd better send these over to Tophet. Tell you what... You deliver them for me."

"I don't think she wants us."

Death chuckled. "Nonsense. You're more of an imposition to me than you are to her." He turned around and walked away. Speaking to the air in front of him, he said, "Give Tophet a message for me. Remind her she can bitch all she wants, but every time she throws a soul back into the world, she makes more work for me. She already knows that, but remind her for me, will you?"

Blaze was getting to know the drill. He held Heather's hand and saw the inevitable flash and smoke, realizing that as soon as it cleared, they'd be back at the Pond of Souls.

CHAPTER THIRTEEN

Tophet sat in front of a smaller cauldron, stirring; the swimming pool and large cauldron were nowhere to be seen. Blaze and Heather stood behind her, and it appeared she didn't know they were there.

"Toe jam! Burnt Liver! Attacking Tarantula! Bat boogers!" She sighed. "No wait. With my luck there would be a bat named Boogers or a tarantula named Attacking."

As Blaze stepped around the chair and stood next to Tophet, she jumped, startled by the arrival. Heather didn't know if she was allowed to speak yet, so she let Blaze do the talking.

"Hi Tophet."

"Oh, you're back. I almost missed you. So...did you ferret out your mission in life?"

"I guess it has something to do with destructivity and not doing Death's job for him. By the way, he said to 'hi' and asked us to give you some souls for him." Blaze held out the handful of rocks.

"Thanks." Tophet took them and without looking, tossed the dried-up souls over her shoulder into the pond.

Heather was relieved Blaze appeared to have some common sense after all and refrained from delivering the real message. Tophet might not appreciate hearing it from a mortal. Or maybe he just forgot. Either way, she was able to breathe freely again. Maybe that's how they were meant to balance and be a good influence on each other? He with assertiveness and she with decorum.

"I guess you've been productive," he said.

"Yes, I managed to finish all the distribution and was getting back to manufacturing a new batch." She laid the spoon against the edge of the cauldron. "I'm sensing one of you has another question for me."

Heather whispered in Blaze's ear.

Tophet tipped her head to one side. "Or do you have something else for Death to clarify? If you do, I'll have to send you back to him."

Heather gasped and looked at Blaze, shaking her head madly while hoping he'd think of something else to say.

"Wait! That's okay. We'll ask him later. Uh…can Heather and I spend some time alone in the grove again?"

Tophet grinned and winked at them. "Be my guest."

Blaze grabbed Heather's hand and led her, hobbling toward the forest.

"Wait!" Tophet cried.

The two of them froze in their tracks and turned around slowly.

"Wouldn't you like to get rid of that clunky thing?" She pointed at Heather's cast.

Heather nodded.

A small puff of smoke surrounded her leg and she felt a cool breeze. As the smoke dissipated, her matched pair of unbroken legs came into view. She tested her now-bare leg's strength by shifting her weight to it, carefully.

"It's all healed, Mortal Number Two. You're good to go." In a poof the crutches disappeared.

Blaze gaped at her legs and then spoke to Tophet. "Why didn't you do that earlier?"

"You didn't ask."

Blaze rolled his eyes, wrapped an arm around Heather's waist and drew her close. "Let's get to that grove." She kissed him on the cheek before they set off in the direction of the forest, holding hands and running.

***

The sun was high in the sky as Blaze reached out, grabbed her waist, and pulled her to his chest. Heather slipped her arms around his neck and emitted a sexy growl. She gently nipped his ear and whispered, "Do any decadent thing you want to me. I'm yours. Body and soul."

Blaze kissed her hair until he reached her cheek, then slid his open mouth down her neck while he kneaded her breasts.

As she worked his t-shirt up his torso, he let go of her sensitive mounds only until she had yanked it over his head. His chest was delightfully hard and well-muscled. Did he work out? There were still things she didn't know about him, but none of it mattered right now.

Blaze pulled her down onto the soft grass and rolled beside her. Propped on his elbow, he swept her hair away from her face. "Do you think we're still under her influence way back here, or do you think it's just us feeling the way we really feel?"

Heather had been wondering the same thing and now that they were Tophet-free, she looked deep into his eyes for a clue. A normal looking light shone out of the brown irises gazing back at her.

"It's hard to say, but I don't think she's controlling us right now." She let out a long sigh. "I'm just glad I can talk freely again."

"Yeah, it's a bummer you have to 'put up and shut up' like that. It can't be easy."

"I'm used to it," she said, resigned.

Blaze rolled onto his back, linked hands behind his head and shifted his focus to the sky. "Well, it ticks me off. I'm going to say something about it."

"Please don't." Heather crawled over him. Bracing her hands on either side of his body, she wedged her face into his line of vision. "She could turn you into a toad or something."

"But then you'd kiss me and turn me into a prince."

"You're already a prince."

"Kiss me anyway."

She leaned closer and before she knew it, his arms were wrapped around her, and they were rolling in the grass. The warmth of his mouth and arms made her melt—his affection more welcome than the right to speak.

She forgot anything she might have wanted to say anyway, while playfully kissing him. Their mouths opened. Their kiss deepened and continued as if it would never stop. Kissing him was like finding an oasis when just about to die of thirst. Her tongue probed his mouth, and his swept around hers. He sucked gently, creating a vacuum that seemed to cement them even closer together. Sharing the same air—and precious little of it—she felt faint but didn't care. She just did the best she could to breathe since air was less important than the feel of his lips.

Minutes later when he eased their lips apart, she felt the loss of the sweet contact. One corner of his mouth curled in an impish smile as he ran his hand up her thigh, under her skirt. A jolt of electricity hit her when his fingers stroked her clit, despite her cotton underpants barring the way.

"Blaze, make love to me. I want you inside me again. Again, and again and again."

Still wearing the same smile, his finger hooked the elastic waist and dragged her panties down while she lifted her bottom. When they were around her knees, she sat up and removed them. With the flimsy cotton bunched up in her fist, she threw them overhand into the woods.

"Let's get you completely naked." He reached around her back, found the clasp on her bra and unfastened it. "How about if you go braless from now on? It might be more comfortable, and I want to be able to touch your pretty breasts any time I want."

"I want you to touch me. You can make love to me anywhere, anytime. Oh, just not in public; that could get you arrested."

He grinned and watched her wriggle out of her skirt while he stripped off his jeans and shirt. "Since we're talking about it, why don't you leave your panties in the woods? I want to be able to flip that skirt up and fuck you at any given moment."

"Wow. That's hot!" She giggled and tossed her bra into the woods too. "There," she said. "Now we're as nude as the day we arrived in this world. Well, the other world I mean."

A fleeting thought passed through her mind that made her wonder if Tophet was working on a solution to get the two of them home, but when Blaze started to touch and caress her naked breasts, her mind went blank. He took one hard nipple into his mouth and suckled. She moaned and arched until he lowered her to the grass. Lying flat on the earth, she concentrated on every nuance of Blaze's loving attention. Consciously experiencing foreplay to the fullest created even more powerful sensations. His mouth applied just the right amount of pressure to each of her nipples in turn. When she arched further into his mouth, he suckled her deeper, setting free a blissful moan which sounded as if it belonged to someone else.

His hand caressed her flat belly as he worked his way down to her curls. Every nerve ending came to life and tingled. Light feathery kisses followed in the wake of his hand until one finger just teased the ridge of her nether lips. She felt her sexual energy flow as he worked his body between her legs. The sun shone down and warmed her skin. This place must be close to heaven.

She parted for him, allowing his mouth to find her vortex. He laved her with his tongue, doing the most wicked things to her. The sensations he wrought intensified as did her moans. When he licked her clit, she howled. Zeroing in on her nub, he sucked, and she thought she'd go crazy. He flicked it with his tongue until Heather began to tremble. Suddenly a wonderful new sensation rolled over her—the most exquisite feeling she had ever experienced in her life. And to think, only a few hours ago she didn't know it could be like this.

She screamed as the sensation of powerful completion surged through her and she shuddered; flashes of light burst across her vision. Orgasm after orgasm washed over her. Trembling, the radiating bliss that rocked her world was even better than before. "Blaze," she cried. "Oh God. Oh my God..."

When she had stopped bucking and her body felt completely boneless and limp, he rose to his haunches and grinned. "You liked that, did you?"

Still trying to come to terms with what had happened, she nodded, panting heavily. Her eyes widened when she noticed his erection, thick and straight and pointing directly at her opening. "I want you," she managed to whisper. "Inside me. I can't wait to feel you inside my...my... vagina."

"Vagina is too clinical, my love." He kissed her tenderly.

"Then what should we call it?"

"You know, some guys call it a c—"

"Don't you dare finish that word!" Heather yelled.

"What? Why not?"

"Because it's the most disgusting word in the English language. People use it as an insult."

"So, what do you suggest? Should we name it?"

"Like what?"

"I don't know...like Cindy?"

"Cindy? That's a stupid name for my love canal," Heather said. "Hey how about Gondola?"

Blaze burst out laughing. "I think I'd be the gondola in your love canal scenario."

"Oh. Right."

"Until we think of something better, I'm just going to fuck you, all right?"

She giggled. "More than all right."

Blaze eased into the ready, aim position while Heather spread her legs wider to welcome him. He held his cock to her opening and slowly sunk his length into her warm, slick center. His girth felt so good, and they both moaned in harmony.

"God, Heather," he said as he thrust in and out. "I love you for letting me do you so much and so often."

"I'm not letting you. I want you to."

"I could fuck you until we die of thirst. Every time I look at you, I want to fuck you."

It wasn't the most romantic thing he could have said, but she didn't care since they were in the middle of her newly discovered favorite activity.

He pumped in a steady rhythm and her hips rose of their own volition to meet him. The deeper he went, the better she liked it. Her moaning increased with the joyous contact of his pelvis against her clit. He used a roll-up motion that was driving her crazy.

She felt the fluttering of another orgasm creep up, about to erupt. She opened her eyes long enough to see Blaze's face. He looked like he was in pain, but his low groans sounded like anything but. At the same time, he began to jerk into her, she felt the contractions of her own delicious spasm spread and increase until she was convulsing in euphoric agony against him. When she had floated on the last wave of her orgasm, she realized her power. She had never felt like this. Now she had...what? Sexual power? Yes. An overwhelming, God-given, natural power meant to be enjoyed when given and happily received.

CHAPTER FOURTEEN

Blaze wanted to get back to the pond to see if Tophet had made any progress. They were just emerging from the forest when he spotted two naked figures going at it on a swing. It didn't take long to figure out it was Tophet and some immortal with a buff build. The ropes holding the swing off the ground weren't anchored to anything but air. Blaze heard Heather gasp and he clapped his hand over her eyes.

She tore his hand away and gaped at the couple fucking like mad, obviously enjoying their zealous frenzy.

"Blaze," she whispered as she continued to stare. "We shouldn't be watching this."

"Why not?" Smiling, his gaze stayed glued to the copulation in progress.

She hit him in the stomach.

Surprised, he stared at her and saw she was visibly fuming. "All right. We can sneak back into the bushes and wait until they're finished."

"I think it would be the polite thing to do," she said.

Blaze settled on the ground with his back against the trunk of the nearest tree and Heather seated herself between his legs. When she leaned against his chest, he automatically cupped her breasts and stroked her nipples with his thumbs.

"Ohh…" she moaned. "I love it when you do that."

"Then I'll keep doing it," he whispered. He ran his lips over her cheek and nibbled her neck as he massaged her mounds. Before long she was writhing and moaning louder. Her pleasure was music to his ears—and music was his favorite thing. Blaze reached between her legs. She was still damp. He slipped his finger between her folds and reached for her start button, gently applying pressure before carefully twisting it. She jerked as if she were a standard transmission thrown into first gear without the clutch in.

She yanked his hand away. "Not here! We're too close. They'll hear us."

The loud moans and deep throaty growls coming from the direction of the swing made him fairly certain their hosts were too involved in their own activities to notice. "Let me make you happy, hon. Just come quietly, okay."

"You sound like a cop: 'Come along quietly and nobody gets hurt'."

Blaze chuckled. "Would handcuffs help?"

Screams of an orgasm like he had never heard before shattered the air from every direction. The cry echoed so loud and so long that they had to clap their hands over their ears or risk permanent hearing loss.

When peace was finally restored, Blaze noticed the same annoying ringing in his ears that usually occurred after his concerts.

"Damn, that woman can amplify!"

"When do you think it will be safe to return?"

"What?" He stuck a finger in his ear and jiggled it, attempting to clear the reception.

"I said, do you think we should give them a few minutes to recover?"

"They might begin round two if we wait."

"Round two? You mean to tell me men can have multiples?" Heather's eyes popped in surprise.

"Sort of." He winked. "We'll eventually get around to that, I promise. I imagine immortals can probably recover faster than us mortals and go at it again and again. I know I would if I could."

He clasped her waist and lifted her off his lap. "Let's see if they're ready for us."

The two of them crept toward the clearing.

"No swing," she whispered. "That's a good sign."

"Come out, come out, wherever you are," Tophet called.

Blaze and Heather straightened. Hand in hand, they emerged from the brush.

Tophet was alone and fully robed. One side of her mouth curled up. "So, you caught me in the act."

"Sorry," Blaze said. "We didn't mean to, but damn it was hard to miss. You're a real screamer!"

Tophet chuckled. "Yeah, that was a good one. It's been a while, you know. So now that I'm in such a good mood, do you have any more questions about reincarnation?"

"Yeah!"

"Fire away."

"I was wondering if either one of us had a really special past life. One in which we accomplished a goal, or learned something we might be able to cross off our list of stuff we have to learn before we're allowed to transcend."

Tophet paused, tipping her head from one side to the other as she thought. After a while, her eyes lit up. "Ah, yes. I can think of an example. You, Mortal Number One, were once the wisest man in China. A respected icon. People traveled from everywhere just to listen to you."

"Really?" Blaze could hardly contain his excitement. "What did I accomplish?"

"You learned from the past, from the mistakes of your ancestors, and you made sure you didn't repeat them. You passed on your wisdom in the I Ching, the oldest book known to mankind. It's existed all this time and still inspires people of the twenty-first century. That's a sign of great wisdom."

"Cool! So, I don't need to learn maturity in this lifetime?"

"You tell me." She grasped her hands behind her back and strolled around him in circles. "You might have carried it over or you might not have. What is your father like?"

Blaze thought about what a good man his father was and hoped he'd see him again someday. "I guess my dad's pretty smart. He has a good job. He worked hard and clawed his way up from the bottom. He's always saying he wants me to have the good things he never had."

"Well, there's your answer. You've obviously learned to do things completely differently from your ancestors."

Heather rolled her eyes.

"Hey! I've just been insulted. I thought you were in a good mood."

Tophet snickered. "I am. I'm enjoying the heck out of myself! Is there anything else you'd like to know?"

"Just one thing. When can we get out of here and go back home?" he asked.

"We're working on it."

He crossed his arms and looked at her askance. "Who's 'we'?"

"Death and I." The swing reappeared and she sat on it.

"Yeah, you two looked like you were working really hard."

Tophet began to pump her feet and said, "You know, I think I should let you go ask Death what he's found out."

Before Blaze could say a word, he heard the familiar poof sound as smoke once again enveloped Heather and him.

CHAPTER FIFTEEN

A hooded Death halted in his tracks just outside a nursing home. He turned slowly when he sensed a new presence behind him only to see Blaze and Heather emerge from the billowing smoke.

"What is this? Mortal ping-pong?"

"Don't blame me. That's how we feel too," Blaze said. "We didn't mean to come back. We just had a question Tophet couldn't answer and poof, here we are."

Death put one hand on his hip and leaned on his scythe. "Okay, what's your question?"

Blaze looked at Heather and she answered for both of them. "Two questions. What about us going home?"

"And your other question?"

"We wanted to know how you can be everywhere at once."

"You mean with people dying all over the globe, how can I take dozens of souls in the same second?"

They nodded in unison.

"I'll answer the second question first. I just can, okay? To answer to your first question, we're working on it."

He began to return to his duties when out of his peripheral vision, he saw Heather whispering something to Blaze.

"What? Excuse me Mortal Number Two? Come here."

"Me?" she squeaked.

"Yes, you. Here. Now."

She started toward him and then stopped suddenly. "Hey, wait a minute. You're going to hit me, aren't you?"

Death folded his arms. "Well, yes. I've been called the original hit man."

Heather backed away. "Oh no you don't. I won't stand for it."

"Suit yourself." He turned away from them and took a few more steps toward the nursing home. As he walked, he heard two slaps and each of them yelled, "Oww!"

"Why did you do that?" Heather squealed.

"Because I can," he answered, without stopping or turning around.

Blaze called out after him, "Then why do you do these one-at-a-time gigs? Do some people get special treatment?"

"Nope. No special treatment, just quality control."

He stopped as he reached the steps and said, "Now does that answer all your silly-ass questions for a while?"

Blaze stuffed his hands in his pockets. "All but one."

Death rolled his eyes and huffed. "Hurry up and get it over with."

"Why the get-up?" he asked, pointing to his robe and scythe.

"Oh, that." Death's smiled gleamed. "Some people still appreciate tradition." He climbed the stairs and paused with his hand on the doorknob. "Listen, why don't you go ask Tophet a question. Ask her why she never sleeps. Go on, trust me, she'll love it."

He waved his hand and with a crack of lightning, sent them back to the pond's edge.

***

When the smoke cleared, they saw Tophet tossing a ball across the lawn, then poofing over to where the ball went to catch it. When she spotted them, she missed a catch and yelled, "Entrails! May armed deer hunt you!" Then as politely as if she were at a tea party, she asked, "Back so soon?"

Blaze sauntered over to her. "Still trying out new profanities?"

"Yes. As you can see, I haven't found the perfect one yet. You'd have heard it by now, believe me."

He tucked his hand into his pocket and asked, "Are we that much of a bother?"

"No, not really." Tophet tossed the ball in the air, and it disappeared. The cauldron materialized in front of her instead. She leaned over it and inhaled deeply. By this time Heather had come up beside Blaze and both of them were riveted to what Tophet was doing.

"Ah... Smell that," Tophet said.

They dutifully bent over the cauldron and sniffed.

While they were distracted, Tophet grabbed her spoon off the lawn, pointed it at them and chanted.

Lust is fun and oh, so nice.
I can't believe you fell for this twice!

Seconds later they were standing in the grove as naked as Adam and Eve.

"For the love of—" Heather's gaze dropped to Blaze's limp rod. She watched it grow and stand up, like a video of a budding daffodil on fast-forward. She looked up into his eyes and saw them smoldering.

"Did you want to say something, lover?" he asked, his voice husky.

She shook her head. "If I did, I forgot what it was."

They fell together in a desperate embrace. Tasting and nipping each other, she was aware of only one thing. She wanted him between her legs, mounting her, pushing his boner into her as soon as possible.

"Oh God, Blaze. Stuff me. Fill me with your cock right now."

He practically wrestled her to the ground and threw his body on top of her. "Baby, if you'll let me, I'm gonna rock your world."

"Let you?" she panted. "I'm begging you!"

He slid his hard body over hers, trailing wet kisses until he reached her breasts. He stopped and sucked one into his mouth like a starving man. The powerful suction sent vibrations rippling right into her womb. Trembling with an impending orgasm, she cried out, arched her back, and burst, screaming her earth-shattering release. She had no idea she could come with only his mouth on her nipple. *Dear God, what does Blaze have in his sexual arsenal?*

He shifted his attention to her other breast and his fingers found her quim. Almost immediately she began bucking while shouting unintelligible sounds as another explosive orgasm hit even before the last one had completely subsided. She shivered and spasmed as her lover rocked her world, just as he had promised.

He gave her only a minute to recover before he slid further down until he was facing her soaking wet curls. He gently separated her labia and extended his tongue, ready to give her the licking of her life.

"Oh God, stop," she begged. She pushed her hands against his forehead, locked her elbows, and held his protruding tongue away from her. "I can't take anymore right now. I'll be your willing lover forever, but please don't give me a heart attack in the process."

He laughed. "Okay. I'll let you rest for a minute, but soon—very soon—I'm going to flip you over and fuck you from behind. Hard and deep. Your pussy's going to beg me to fill it all the way to your G-spot from now on."

Panting too hard to answer, she managed a smile and a nod, but had no idea what he was talking about.

Before she knew it, Blaze grabbed her by her shoulder and hip and rolled her onto her stomach.

She giggled as she tried to bat him away. "Wait; don't you want me to go down on you?"

"I'm hard as a rocket, baby. Right now, I just want to ride you into the stratosphere."

"Stratosphere? Where's that?"

"I don't know, but we'll find out together."

He wedged an arm under her belly and yanked her up onto her hands and knees with one pull. She couldn't stop giggling. It was a nervous laugh, but she was anxious to find out what he was talking about. She'd do anything her lover asked of her at this point. If he wanted her to stand on her head and suck honey off his balls, she'd do it. She just wished she wasn't so naïve.

He positioned himself behind her, but before he entered her, he ran his hands over her bum. "You have the finest ass, Heather. I'm gonna fuck that too someday."

"What are you going to do to me right now?" she teased, waving her buttocks at him.

He groaned. "I'm gonna stick my big, hard dick into you and diddle your clit while I fuck you up the stairway to heaven."

She moaned at the image his words conjured up and parted her damp thighs. She couldn't wait. It was as if she had been made specifically to receive his most personal part and cherish everything he did to her with it. But that's love...right? His firm tip prodded her entrance. Without warning he plunged into her fast and deep then didn't move. Incredible sensations filled her. She experienced a deep satisfaction in her body, mind, and soul, knowing she was filled with the one puzzle piece that made her complete. Yes, he belonged there. She needed him inside of her like she needed food in her stomach—maybe more.

Thinking of food at time like this is ridiculous, isn't it? Then she remembered they hadn't eaten all day. Plenty of sexercise but no food. Well, they'd deal with that later. Right now, Blaze was pulling back almost all the way, and then thrusting in as far as he could go. Delicious torture!

She wanted him so much and yet she was convinced he was going to drive her mad. Once he settled into a hard but consistent rhythm she could match, she pushed her well-lubricated sheath backward over his shaft as he thrust into her. His balls slapped against her butt as he held her hips in his strong grasp and drove in and out of her like a piston. Each thrust was so deep he always connected with what must have been her G spot. She felt an intense force looming up inside of her until a deep bubble of unbelievable ecstasy burst, sending her into a starry, hard, almost violent orgasm. As her muscles contracted and clenched his cock, he grunted and dug his fingers into her flesh. When she had climaxed all the way to the stratosphere, ionosphere and beyond, shards of her former self lay scattered over the ground.

If this was what sex with one's soul mate was like, she felt positively blessed to have found him early in life. She wanted to fuck him senseless for the next seven decades.

"Wow, you came for me so easily and I never even touched your clit, Heather."

"Then fuck me again. Up the ass this time, while you rub my clit."

"Holy... Are you sure?"

She just grinned.

CHAPTER SIXTEEN

Tophet had just finished her last toss and was wiping her hands on a towel. Heather and Blaze were crouching in the tall grass, watching for a good opportunity to interrupt the touchy immortal.

Blaze stood and covered his privates with his hands. "Excuse me, can we have our clothes back now?"

Tophet snickered. "Of course."

One poof later, the mortals were clothed and emerged into the clearing.

"You didn't have to make us that hot for each other, you know," Blaze said. "We'd have gone willingly, especially since there doesn't seem to be much we can do to help you."

Tophet pulled out a pocket watch. "Yeah, you're right. I felt like I needed plenty of time to get the next batch out, though."

Heather braced a hand on the grass and gingerly sat down.

"Feeling a bit less virginal now, Mortal Number Two?"

Heather cleared her throat and adjusted her position until she was comfortable.

Blaze sat next to her and stroked her thigh. "I think she could use a break. In the meantime, we have another question for you."

"Of course, you do. What is it?"

"How come you never sleep?"

Heather shook her head furiously at Blaze. Why the heck did he ask that? She wanted to know when and how they were going home!

"Well now, I'm going to make you guess." Tophet tossed her head, acting smug.

There was a long pause in which Blaze looked as if he were puzzling over the question. Heather dropped her head into her hands and hoped the man of her dreams didn't say something to get himself killed.

"I've got it," he said at last. "You drink too much caffeine."

Tophet's eyes grew wide. Filled with a psychotic look, she straightened to her full height, took an aggressive stance, and yelled. "I know that!"

Blaze leaned toward Heather and shielded her body. "You didn't have to get so hostile about it."

They watched silently as Tophet struggled to regain control. "Wow, I wonder where that came from?"

Heather continued to stare at her and hoped she'd read her mind.

Tophet clasped her hands behind her back and started pacing. "Yes, I've been giving a lot of thought to how you got here. I think it might shed some light on how to send you back."

Blaze flinched. "Are you planning to strap us to your boomerang and throw us?"

"Of course not, Mortal Number One. You'd just come back again. No, I think there must have been more to it than my boomerang. There had to be some cosmic interference from your side. I mean, look…" She stopped pacing and pointed to the pond. "I'm tossing stuff into your dimension all the time, and this has never happened before. Someone who didn't know what they were doing must have managed to make a poof on the other side, and voila, here you are.

Blaze and Heather looked at each other, confused.

"But who could that be?" Blaze asked.

"My guess is an uninitiated, under-trained, new witchlet had to be fooling around with some advanced magic. Something he or she shouldn't have even attempted."

"What?" Blaze raised his eyebrows. "Are you saying we got here by magic?"

"It sure beats the heck out of any other theories I've heard so far. By the way, if you come up with anything positive to contribute, feel free to share. Otherwise, please refrain from pissing me off by doubting everything I say."

Blaze scratched his head, a look of concentration on his face as he stared at the grass in front of him. Heather wracked her brain to come up with something more plausible too. Finally, the two of them shrugged.

"Okay," Blaze said. "That's probably what happened. Now what?"

Tophet held out her hands and produced a thick tome with a beat-up leather binding. She blew on the top of it and a cloud of dust flew into the air.

"I found a very old, reliable spell-book. It contains a complicated spell to reverse spells that backfire. It's called the 'do-over spell'."

Blaze opened his mouth to speak but must have thought better of it and shut it, fast.

"Good for you for not doubting me, Mortal Number One. Now why don't you look it up?"

She tossed the heavy book Blaze's way and it landed with a thud on the ground in front of him. Another dust cloud rose, this time reaching his face. He coughed and began sneezing, waving his hand to try to dissipate the irritants.

"Oh, I forgot about that dust allergy. Here, I'll find it for you." She waved her hand and the pages flipped until the book lay open to a page with beautiful calligraphy. Heather focused on the heading at the top of the page. 'Do over spell' was written with a flourish that would have made a monk proud.

Tophet came up behind the mortals and leaned over their shoulders. She stared down at the book and muttered, "There are more ingredients here than in low-fat salad dressing!"

She studied it a moment and asked the mortals, "You got any wolf hair?"

"Not since the last full moon," Blaze quipped.

Tophet walked back to where she stood before, shaking her head. "If you could only come up with bad words as easily as you come up with bad jokes..."

Blaze returned to the matter at hand to Heather's relief. "It's kind of like a recipe, isn't it? I hear my mom talking about substituting ingredients all the time. Maybe we could find something else to use for wolf's hair, like dog hair?"

Tophet heaved a huge sigh. "Dear, dear Mortal Number One. Your idiocy is only exceeded by your dangerous good intentions. Such substitutions are only for trained professionals."

She hung her head and shook it at the ground, then straightened up as if she had thought of something brilliant. "I know. You can ask Death! He knows more about this kind of stuff than I do."

Blaze held his hands up in a 'stop' gesture. "That might be dangerous too. I don't think he likes us anymore."

"Don't be silly," she said. "He never did, but don't let that stop you." She tore the page from the book and folded it. "Here, give this to him and let him know what it's for. He wants to send you back as badly as I do. Good luck!"

The inevitable poof and cloud of smoke enveloped the two mortals again. Blaze swore.

The smoke cleared and they found themselves standing behind Death in what looked like a dentist's office. Death stood behind a man who was on his knees.

"Shh... Don't make a sound. He might still change his mind."

They watched in horror as the man raised a gun to his own mouth and pulled the trigger.

"Crap!" Death took the brunt of the man's blood right in his face. Sighing, he turned toward the mortals and wiped his face on the long, loose sleeves of his black robe. "Well, I'm glad I wore my rubber gloves."

"You're being sarcastic, right?" Blaze asked.

"Right."

Heather gripped her throat. "What just happened?"

"That, my little mortal, was a suicide. What a pity." Death shook his head.

"Why? Just because it makes more work for you?" Heather turned away from the body and huddled in Blaze's arms. How she would've handled this without his quiet strength, she didn't know.

"No. I can understand it in some cases. This was not one of them, though. This was about a woman." Death 'tsk, tsked' and walked to the sink. "If he had just realized his pain would pass, his life would've worked out better as a result of losing her."

Death washed his face and then discarded his gloves and robe in the red bag. Heather was surprised to see him wearing casual pants and a striped shirt underneath.

He huffed and shook his head. "So why are you back, my persistent new friends?"

"We need your help with something," Blaze said.

"Before that, though," Heather interjected. "Can we talk about that sad man and what you meant by his life would have been better because of losing her?"

"Sure, but let's go into the waiting room to talk. Even I don't like the look of brains on the floor."

Heather almost threw up.

"You go first. I'll gather his soul and be there in a minute."

The couple entered the waiting room with Heather breathing deeply and rubbing her arms to try to wipe the chill away. Death joined them a few seconds later.

"So Mortal Number Two, what did you want to know?"

"Well, it sounds like he had a choice. I thought fate was fate."

"Oh no. He certainly had a choice there. Did you see me interfering?"

They both shook their heads.

"Of course not. And to answer your earlier question, yes, it does make more work for me." Death tossed the man's soul in the air and caught it.

"But his soul looks all shriveled and used up. Maybe he was at the end anyway and somehow, he just knew it?"

Death stopped playing catch with the man's soul and frowned at Heather. "Maybe. How should I know? Why are you always asking me Tophet's questions and asking her mine? You should ask her about that."

Heather hung her head. "She doesn't want me to talk at all."

"I'd return you, but she'd just bounce you right back to me." He shrugged and patted her on the shoulder. "Did you say there was something you needed help with?"

"Yeah," Blaze piped up. "We need a few things for a reversal spell." He pulled out the list and handed it to Death.

"A reversal spell? For yourselves? As in counteracting some crazy spell gone awry and getting the hell out of here?"

"Yeah. We don't have all the ingredients and she said you know more about substitution than she does. Can you help?"

Death wrinkled his brow and leaned back in the comfortable upholstered blue chair, reading the list. His eyes rounded.

"Are you sure Tophet isn't up to some kind of practical joke?"

"No. She seemed to be on the level."

Death shook his head at the list. "This is nonsense. Eye of Newt? Oh, come on, give me a break. What does she want me to do, pop down to Newts R Us? Or order one from newts.com? I'm sure it's a joke. She has an oddball sense of humor, you know, even if it's a bit cliché.

Death held out his hand and a copy of Playboy appeared with a light poof. He opened the magazine and tore out a small circle. "Here's your substitution. Call it 'eye of nude.' It's almost exactly the same thing."

Blaze looked at the tiny picture. "But..."

"No buts. Who are you going to believe?" Pointing to himself, he said, "Mr. Bottom-line?" Or... He used his index finger to make circles around his ear. "Or a fanciful female still looking for the perfect curse word?"

Blaze groaned and Heather grimaced, knowing this trip had been no help at all.

"Okay," she said. "We'll take it to her, but don't be surprised if we crop up again."

Death snorted. "I'm breathless with anticipation."

CHAPTER SEVENTEEN

Tophet was stretched out on her recliner, reading the Universal Enquirer. As the smoke cleared, she managed to stuff the paparazzi rag into the breast pocket of her robe and pull out a copy of Reincarnation Today. Casually, she remarked, "Oh, hello. What did you find?"

Blaze handed her the small scrap of paper that showed only an eye.

She squinted at it and said, "Miss January. The eyes are the windows to the soul. Ah, yes. Pretty eyes, but you should have seen the rest of her without the nose job, breast enhancements, lipo and makeup. Of course, they airbrushed the photo too."

"Death said it was a substitution for eye of newt."

"Dry heaves and dead leaves! Eye of nude? Was that all he could come up with? Doesn't he realize what this means?"

Blaze shrugged. "I don't know. He said you were setting us up with a practical joke."

"I'm afraid not. I don't joke and he knows it. I get sarcastic and sassy, but I'm not a practical joker. That's his shtick. We've been had."

"So, you're saying we're back to square one?"

"Unless you can come up with any brilliant ideas." She rolled her eyes. "Look who I'm talking to."

"Hey! I thought you made me more intelligent. Unless you don't believe in your—"

Tophet waved away his words and rose from her recliner. A moment later it disappeared into thin air. She began to pace then stopped and glared at the mortals. "You two can take a nap if you're still tired or sore from your last trip to the grotto. I need to think."

Blaze looked at Heather and she nodded. "Okay, where should we go?"

"Oh, poop. I forgot that you need me to provide you with absolutely everything."

"Um…Tophet? Speaking of providing stuff. Can we have something to eat?"

Tophet slapped her forehead. "Horse tails and entrails."

The mortals' eyes widened. Blaze leaned toward her and whispered, "You don't have to cook or anything, but you aren't really going to give us that to eat, are you?"

"That was another expletive, Mortal Number One. Of course, if you'd like…"

Blaze hastily held up both of his hands and stepped back. "No! Don't. Do you have any real food we might like? We'd be very thankful if you could conjure up something. We're starving."

"Thankful, huh?" Tophet produced her spoon and pointed it at an empty space. She poofed up a table and two chairs, complete with a white tablecloth and full course turkey dinner. It smelled pretty good too. Mortals had all the fun sometimes.

Heather and Blaze sat at the table and Tophet could almost see their mouths watering. They put their napkins in their laps and Heather looked up at Tophet. Blaze was about to shovel food onto his plate when Heather kicked him under the table. He stopped what he was doing and looked over at her.

She jerked her head toward Tophet a couple of times while maintaining eye contact with him.

"Oh! Would you like to join us, Tophet?"

Tophet smiled for a millisecond and put on her scowl again. "No thanks."

"Are you sure? It looks really good and—"

"Immortals don't eat." She crossed her arms feeling somewhat superior.

"Do they go to the bathroom?"

Heather kicked him under the table again.

"What's the matter?" he said. "I want to know. I have extra room in my head for knowledge now. Why not use it for a little immortal trivia?"

Tophet smirked. "Nothing in, nothing out."

"That's cool," Blaze said. "Maybe you can conjure up a port-a-potty later? Save us a trip to the woods?"

Tophet threw her hands in the air and stormed over to them. "Do you want to move in, or do you want to get home? Better decide before you waste all my time with your silly little creature comforts."

"Okay, okay. Forget it."

Heather passed the sweet potatoes and reached for the rolls at the same time.

More souls plummeted from the sky into the water. Tophet wandered over to the bank of the pond and gazed into it. Meanwhile a number of souls were floating to the top, indicating they were ready to be sent back. Tophet clenched her fists and muttered, "Oh, maggot sundaes with puss on top."

Ewww.

"I think I've lost my appetite," Blaze said.

Tophet whirled around and glared at them with her fists and jaw clenched. "I made it; so you'll eat it!" She wasn't kidding.

"We're eating, we're eating!" Blaze shoveled a large forkful of food into his mouth, chewed twice and then mumbled around the mouthful, "It's delicioush."

After chowing down on a big turkey dinner with all the fixings and washing that down with tall glasses of cold milk, Heather and Blaze got up from the table and stretched. Blaze finished up with a long yawn and a loud burp.

Delighted, Tophet was stirring her cauldron and snickering. She congratulated herself for coming up with a Tryptophan-loaded meal. A natural enzyme that makes them drowsy is better than knocking them out. She pointed her spoon in front of the couple and a bed appeared in place of the table.

"Oh, yeah," Blaze said. "That's more like it. I could really use a nap about now. Thanks Tophet."

She waved and called out, "No problem. Why don't you lie down and rest your eyes?"

The mortals collapsed on the bed, not even bothering to pull the covers over themselves. They were asleep in seconds.

Tophet dropped her spoon and wandered over to them. She clasped her hands behind her back and circled the bed, never taking her eyes off of them. "Dear God and Goddess. How am I going to get rid of them? I should hate myself for what I'm thinking."

A low voice in the distance rumbled. "I dare you to do it."

"Death? Is that you?"

"Who else would it be?" The voice, now clear, was right behind her.

She whirled around. "Oh, Death. Am I glad to see you!"

He folded his arms and cocked his head. "You can't do it, can you?"

They both looked at the bed holding the two sleeping souls, breathing in, and snoring out. She shook her head. "No, I can't. It's so Jonestown. How do you do it? How can you tell when it's the last resort?"

Staring at her, unblinking, he was silent for several seconds. One corner of his lip curled, making him look annoyingly smug. "I bet you think I'm here to help you."

"I was hoping…"

He lifted his chin and stared down his nose at her. "And what would that accomplish? Would you feel empowered? Proud of yourself? Would being rid of a temporary annoyance be worth the crushing guilt you'd have to live with for, well, forever?"

"I don't like where this is going."

He seemed to grow and loom over her. His eyes narrowed and blackened. "If you start treading on my turf, you're going to get yourself in a lot of trouble."

Tophet took a step back then planted her feet firmly on the ground. Refusing to be intimidated, she set her hands on her hips and looked up into his menacing face. "What are you getting at?"

Death shrunk to his normal size and circled around her. He seemed to be studying her. "I can see I'm going to have to get this across in a way you'll understand." He cleared his throat and broke into song.

Death is serious business.
Amateurs need not apply.
How would you know
the way they should go?

When to freeze and when to fry?

Death is serious business.
You might take them out with a bang.
How would you know
the way they should go?
Shark bite or quietly hang?

Death is serious business.
What, were you just gonna guess?
How would you know
the way they should go?
And accidents make such a mess.

There are so many various choices,
I sometimes get boggled myself.
To strangle, to crush, or to poison,
or mix up the medicine shelf?

You know those so-called freak accidents?
The ones you can hardly believe?
Well, that in itself should be telling you
I have many tricks up my sleeve.

Yes, Death is serious business.
Amateurs, leave it alone.
I am the only professional.
Well, only me and my clone.

Death faced Tophet and glared at her. "Stay out of my 'hood. You don't know what you're doing, so leave them alone."

She shivered inwardly but nodded and held her composure. "You're probably right. I might have made a big mistake."

"Well, as much as that would have been fun to watch, I couldn't let you do it. I don't think you took the time to consider the consequences. It's so tempting to go for the fastest solution to a problem, but..." He strolled behind her, put his hands on her shoulders and kissed her neck. "You're just feeling stressed right now, baby. Let me relax you."

CHAPTER EIGHTEEN

He massaged her shoulders and she let her head fall forward, sighing her pleasure at his touch. His strong grip moved over her neck and then he nuzzled her wherever his hands had been, his hot breath and talented kneading extracted moans of pleasure. He traced circles over her upper back and along her shoulders blades until his wandering hands traveled around to her chest and massaged her mounds. As he manipulated her nipples she trembled and let out a heartrending sound, as if craving unmet fulfillment.

"Does that help, Toffee baby?"

"Oh yes," she purred. "That feels very good."

He trailed kisses down her neck from ear to collarbone. While one hand worked her breasts, lightly pinching her nipples whenever his fingers grazed one, his other hand slid lower and found her crotch.

"Oh!" She threw her head back, pulled her robe open and pushed her pelvis into his big, hot hand. She was wet with need and her clenching chasm ached to have him inside of her. "Please...I need you!"

His breath tickled as he whispered into her ear. "I want to fuck you, baby. I want to lay you down and kiss, lick and suck you. I want to make you come a hundred times."

"Ohh…" she moaned. After a few more seconds of glorious torture, she stepped away from him. She let her robe fall to the ground and turned around, displaying her nakedness. She was so ripe. Her nipples were turgid peaks one could hang a hat on. Her legs glistened at the tops of her thighs, and that could only mean one thing.

He stripped off his robe before claiming her lips in passionate possession. They devoured each other's mouths while they stroked each other's bodies and genitals. When they fell over, instead of hitting the ground they hovered a few inches above it.

Death cupped and squeezed her ass. He was almost breathless as he whispered, "We should go somewhere more private, in case the kids wake up. They might be traumatized."

No sooner had Tophet nodded her agreement, than the two of them floated over the pond to the other side, kissing, nipping, and sucking all the while. Once there, a blanket materialized beneath them, and they gently lowered themselves onto it. Death adjusted his position so he could pull her nipple into his mouth and suckle her. The happiest of tingly sensations from his suckling shot throughout her nerve endings, causing her body to writhe. Her vaginal walls clenched, big time. Her creamy cunt signaled her readiness to accept his stiff erection, but the torture of his slow, patient foreplay was worth the delay.

She let him thrill her, sucking, licking, and nipping each of her breasts soundly before he moved on to her aching clit. He flicked his tongue over it. She arched her back and trembled, moaning her rapture. "Make me come, honey. I'm so horny and I want to come so bad. Make me come in your mouth."

"I want you to," he said. "Over and over." He took her swollen clit between his eager lips and sucked. She vibrated and screamed as her climax broke, spreading delicious spasms throughout her body. She continued to tremble and moan with blissful release. When, at last, she didn't think she could stand any more pleasure, she begged him, "Stop, please stop. I can't...I mean...no more."

He released her, grinning, and her words were lost on a sigh.

Letting her recover momentarily, he wiped his mouth with the back of his hand. As soon as she was breathing normally, he flopped over onto his back and rested his hands behind his head. Of course, he appeared cocky, but maybe he had a right to feel that way.

It felt as if she had no bones and muscle to move, as if her body had turned to rubber. She took a couple of deep lungfuls of air and glanced at his engorged hard-on. His rod stood up like a sign saying, 'full speed ahead', awaiting her attention.

Tophet dragged herself up onto one elbow and stroked his hard phallus while trying to recover her strength. "That was incredible. Have you been reading sex manuals or something?"

He chuckled. "Or something."

Wrong answer. Jealous thoughts about the Moon Goddess popped into her head. She grasped his swollen, well-veined, purple penis, squeezing a little harder than necessary, and pondered her next move.

He groaned. She wasn't sure if it was pleasure or pain, but she concluded she'd do whatever it took to knock out the competition. He'd be horny for her and only her if it meant she had to stand on her head while he fucked her upside-down.

She dove for his erection and nearly swallowed it whole.

He gasped and arched his back. "Take it easy, Toffee baby! I'm going to need that for later."

She turned on the suction, withdrew, and was gratified by his deep moan. When she reached the end of his full nine inches, she let the swollen tip pop out of her mouth. "I guess the Moon Goddess was all soft and gentle, huh? Is that how you like it?"

Death raised himself up on his elbows. "Is that what you think?"

"Well, for scum's sake Death, you said 'or something'… What am I supposed to think?"

He flopped back on the blanket and blew out a long breath. "I meant that you inspire me."

"Is that a line?"

Death pressed the palms of his hands over his eyes and growled.

"What's the matter?"

He struggled to sit up then stroked her hair. "Why is it so hard for you to believe you're still attractive to me? I'm crazy about you, baby. It never used to be this difficult. It took a wink to get you horny and a minute of foreplay to get you off. We could have done it ten times a day if we didn't have jobs."

Tophet smiled at the memory. "Yeah."

"Well, why don't we give it all we've got to get that back?"

"I want to…"

He tackled her and pinned her to the ground. "Good." He nuzzled her neck, making her laugh while he nudged her legs apart with his knee. He lowered his mouth to hers and kissed her hungrily, as if he wanted to devour her. He grasped and held her hands over her head.

She felt his penis prod her opening and raised her pelvis to encourage and welcome him. Desperately wanting to sheath him, she hoped he'd be able to get his cock inside her with no hands. Heat flooded her as she pictured him fucking her hard while holding her down. A rush of fluid buttered her passage, and he pushed his cock smoothly into her.

"Ohh..." she moaned. "You feel so good." His glowing life essence filled her. For an immortal, that meant a lot. Life was endless...forever.

He still had her wrists pinned to the ground and didn't let them go as he pumped in and out. "It does feel good, doesn't it baby? Fucking you just makes me want to fuck you more. You're addictive. I can't get enough of you. I want to fuck you ten times a day. Job, or no job."

She moaned and melted into the rhythm of their bodies mating. This had to be the most intense experience of her life so far—and that was saying something!

He increased the intensity of his thrusts, making her quiver with each enthusiastic drive. The rippling sensations of an impending orgasm reverberated from her core, outward to all of her sensitive nerve endings until she erupted in ecstasy. Her clenching muscles must have set off his orgasm. Death followed her release close behind, grunting as his body jerked.

They lay still coupled together, breathing fast for a nice, cuddly, long while. When they separated and lay next to each other, Tophet reached for his hand. They fit their fingers together and other than their deep breathing, their bodies lay immobilized.

It had been a long time since Tophet had felt so feminine and desired. It had been even longer since she had been so deeply satisfied.

Come to think of it, she didn't have the slightest urge to swear at anyone or anything now. Note to self: Must do this more often. Need for bad words might diminish.

***

"I could stay here and screw all afternoon, but I've gotta get back to work, baby."

"Yeah, me too."

Death stood and poofed back to the side of the pond where their tryst had begun. He lifted his black cape off the grass and slipped into it. Tophet followed him and found her own robe in a heap. She shook it out and poofed it on.

Death looked over at the mortals who were spooning and sleeping peacefully in their four-poster bed. "I'm glad they slept so soundly so we could have our fun."

She strolled up beside her lover and rubbed his back. "A big turkey dinner will do it every time. Now maybe they'll stop complaining about all their annoying, human needs like eating and sleeping for a while."

Death leveled his gaze at her. "You can't be upset with them for that. They have to take care of those needs, or they'll meet me much earlier than necessary."

She shrugged. "I guess you're right. It's no wonder they don't have a problem with boredom like I do. Every day is gobbled up by eight hours of sleep, working to make money, three meals and going to the bathroom. How do they find time to make love?"

"I don't know. I think they'd be happier if they managed to fit it in more often. Just a theory," Death said, and he winked.

Tophet thought of a question she had never asked him before. "What's it like when their number is up during the sex act?"

Death laughed. "Oh, those are my favorite deaths. They come—and then go—with smiles on their faces, and oh, how I love to watch!"

"Do you watch when you don't have to be there?"

"Of course not! I'm not a pervert!"

"Oh." Tophet pasted an innocent smile on her face.

Blaze stretched and yawned as he awoke. His cock accidentally bumped up against Heather's ass, and she roused with a smile on her face.

Death and Tophet disappeared then materialized behind a tree a few feet away. Neither one of them was about to pass up a front row seat.

Heather peeked around and seeing no one, rolled toward Blaze. Cupping his balls, she whispered, "You want more?"

He grinned. "Absolutely. Take your clothes off, Heather. Slowly. Let me watch you do a strip tease for me."

She giggled and slid off her side of the bed while Blaze propped himself on his elbow.

"I've never done this before. Don't laugh at me, okay?"

"I'd never laugh at you, sweetheart. Do you want me to sing to get you in the mood?"

"No, better not. I don't want to attract Tophet's attention."

Tophet slapped a hand over her mouth and muffled her snicker.

As Heather swayed, slowly unzipping the back of her skirt, the hem swished suggestively. Her hips circled as if she were playing with a hula-hoop in slow motion and her skirt slid off. As soon as she was naked from the waist down, she unbuttoned her blouse and held it open. She faced him and shimmied, making her boobs wiggle suggestively.

"Oh yeah, baby," Blaze said. "I love to see your tits bounce. Now lose the blouse and do a little a little bump and grind for me."

While Heather complied, Blaze yanked off his t-shirt, jeans, and briefs. She lowered her body down behind the bed and then popped up like she was the girl in the cake at a bachelor party. She turned to tease him with peeks at her ass. Blaze may have been erect already, but now his hard-on felt like a pulsating rock.

Now that she was completely naked, she danced provocatively around one of the bedposts. She proceeded to the one closest to his face and did the same thing but reached out to stroke his face and chest, pulling out of his reach each time he tried to grab her.

Eventually he managed to reach her pussy and diddle her clit. She reared back and cried out but let him continue. When violent shivers and moans made it look like she was going to come standing up, she climbed back on the bed and straddled him.

Without waiting for any more foreplay, she lowered and impaled herself on his cock. Leaning forward to brush her nipples back and forth over his chest, she asked, "Did you like that, sweetheart? My stripping for you?" She increased the speed as she bounced up and down on Blaze's cock and he moaned.

Death stepped out from behind the tree. "Oh yeah. Ride him cowgirl!"

Heather screamed, covered her breasts with her hands and stared wide-eyed at the two immortals watching them.

"Fuck," Blaze yelled. "What do you think you're doing?"

Death crossed his arms and leaned against the tree. "Watching you get some. What else did you think we were doing?"

"Ruining the mood, dude!"

"Don't be so self-conscious," Tophet interjected.

"Don't be so freakishly nosy," Heather fired back.

Death sighed. "I guess if nothing's going to happen now, I may as well leave."

"Yes, please do," Heather said, her voice shaking.

CHAPTER NINETEEN

She was still sitting atop Blaze's dick when Death disappeared.

Tophet shook her head. "Mortal Number Two, I can understand your frustration since Mortal Number One's winky is wilting, but you can't talk to me like that. I asked you not to speak before, didn't I? Now I'm going to have to give you a gag order."

"A—a what?"

"I'm ordering you to stop talking, or I'll do it for you. Your voice annoys me. From now on, don't speak unless you're specifically asked to."

"Shit," Blaze said. "Her voice is cute. What's the matter? You can dish out criticism like there's no tomorrow, but you can't take it?"

"Careful, Mortal Number One. You have no idea how close you are to having no tomorrow."

Blaze and Heather grasped each other, and Heather whispered furiously in his ear.

"That's bullshit," he said.

More frantic whispering ensued, and Tophet yawned, getting bored.

"Look, you two. I have some paperwork to do. Now why don't you get dressed and try to find a newt."

Blaze raised his eyebrows. "What kind of paperwork could you have?"

Heather elbowed him and pointed to their clothes.

"Oh. Tophet, would you mind turning your back for a second?"

Tophet whirled around in a circle and poofed the mortals back into their clothes.

Blaze jumped off the bed, adjusted his jeans and helped a blushing Heather down. As soon as her feet hit the ground the bed disappeared.

"So, what kind of paperwork?" he repeated. "I thought you said you had nothing to type or file."

Tophet crossed her arms and looked off into the horizon. "Oh, you know. Boring stuff really. You wouldn't be interested."

"Yes, I would"

Tophet looked down and kicked the grass. "Oh, it's just some quality control stuff." In an almost inaudible voice she admitted, "I have to record my mistakes."

Blaze's face brightened. "Mistakes? You make mistakes? What kind of mistakes?"

This could be embarrassing. "Mistakes. You know, bloopers, outtakes, practical jokes that backfire..."

Heather and Blaze gaped at each other.

"What? You thought immortals were perfect?" Tophet smirked. "Here's an example."

A giant ledger appeared in her hands. She opened it and flipped through several pages until she found the entry she wanted. "Once I made the mistake of trying to handle too much at once. Death was busy during the crusades, so years later, when all those souls were ready to go back at once, it got very busy for me."

"What did you do?"

"I lost track of which souls I had sent where and threw two souls into the same body."

Heather gasped.

"Hey, the kid grew up to be a doctor. I thought I was in the clear until Mrs. Jekyll freaked out."

Blaze chuckled. "That was you, huh? What other types of mistakes do you have in there?"

"What am I? Your own personal gag reel? Would you like to see the home video version?"

"Yeah, that'd be cool."

Tophet shrugged. "Tough, there isn't one. In case you didn't notice I was being sarcastic, but I can see that isn't going to discourage you." She scanned the pages. "Ah, here's one. A young woman who was very cruel when it came to taunting the disabled needed to learn a lesson, so I tried to return her as a scapegoat."

"Uh oh. What did you do? Turn her into a goat?"

Tophet laughed. "Yeah. She was still wearing her hoop earrings. You should have seen the surprise on my face. The more I thought about it, the harder I laughed. So, I left her that way. Then she could see what it felt like to be gawked at."

"I thought you were only able to reincarnate people?"

Tophet shrugged. "I thought so too. It must have been some sort of technical glitch at the time."

"But you could have turned her back? You said you left her that way..." Blaze squinted and frowned.

Tophet sighed. "Yeah. There's a five second rule. If I discover a mistake within the first five seconds of a soul entering its body, I can still grab it back."

Blaze nodded. "Like when an Oreo cookie falls on the floor."

Tophet stared at him in complete non-understanding, but he didn't seem to notice. Screw it.

"Tell us another one."

Heather poked him in the side, and he looked over at her scowling face. He figured he needed to be somewhat understanding. "Hopefully, someone you didn't hurt too much?"

"I don't hurt anyone. I humble them."

"Is humility the way to overcome destructivity?"

"It's a good start," Tophet said. "But sometimes there are people who are too humble. I've made a few mistakes with them too."

Blaze looked so excited at the prospect of a whole new category of errors in judgment, she thought he might start jumping up and down. "Like what? Tell us."

"You really love it when I embarrass myself, don't you?"

"Well, yeah."

"Just one more and I don't even need to look this one up. This mistake was one of my worst." Tophet closed the book and poofed it away. She clasped her hands behind her back and paced back and forth. "Did you ever wonder how a whole group of people who were terribly humbled, more like humiliated, would overcome that in a future life?"

Blaze nodded. "Now that you mention it."

"Okay, well there was this whole group of people from a large war...I needed to give them some of their fight back—some spunk. Particularly the women. They had been treated horribly."

Blaze cocked his head, worried. "Uh oh. What did you do?"

"I invented PMS."

Heather burst into tears, pulled a box of Midol out of her pocket and threw it at Tophet.

"Hey! I didn't say I was proud of it. Mistakes are meant to be forgiven. Furthermore, it looks like the only mistake I'm making now is wasting a colossal amount of time and getting nothing done."

She sat and slumped forward, her chin resting heavily in her palm. As usual, a seat, this time a rock, appeared under her butt at the right moment. "Maybe I'll just say, 'to hell with it', as you would Mortal Number One and do what I want at this point. Maybe I'll sing."

"Is that what you like to do?" Blaze asked. "Sing?"

"Sometimes. I enjoy painting even more."

He looked around. "Can we see some of your paintings?"

Tophet stood straight and proud, like she was feeling a little better and hoping to show off her good side. "Well, I'm not a professional or anything like that, but I guess I could show you some of my work." She swept her arm in a wide arc. The pond and sky turned dark with a hint of blue, the sun just peeking over the horizon. In a loud voice she announced, "The Pond at Dawn."

Her arm rose until she was pointing directly above her head. The sky brightened and the sun rose until it was directly overhead. The colors became more vibrant and the landscape clearer. "The Pond at Noon!"

When she swung her arm down the other way, the sun dipped behind the trees. The sky turned into differing shades of pink and orange. She nodded her approval. "The Pond at Sunset."

Crossing her arms, she looked over at the mortals. "I find creativity so rewarding."

Blaze rolled his eyes. "If you say so."

"What? When Monet did it, they called him brilliant!" Tophet jammed her hands on her hips and leaned forward aggressively.

"Ah...yeah. Hey, can we visit Death again?"

"Visit Death? Why would you want to do that? Is he more interesting? Wittier? Cooler?"

Blaze saw Death appear behind Tophet but didn't point him out. Death didn't appear anxious to announce his presence, either. He just leaned against the tree and listened. Heather and Blaze glanced at each other. Blaze thought it best to answer the simmering immortal's question.

"No! Not at all. We just want to learn more about the destructivity stuff he was telling us about. It sounded like it was important, and I didn't really understand it completely the first time he tried to explain it."

Tophet relaxed her posture and nodded. "Fine, that's something I can help with. You don't need to go to bothering Death about it. I don't know how tolerant he is, and I don't want to be there when he runs out of patience."

"He already slapped us," Blaze said.

Heather rubbed her cheek.

"Oh? Better not chance it then. Your souls aren't ready for the consequences."

"What do you mean?"

"I've never had the courage to ask him, but it can't be good...I guess he resents the extra work."

Blaze noticed Death's brows knit. His expression turned from a sardonic smirk to a frown.

"We have a special contract that forces me to..."

Death leaned forward on his scythe, his look one of confusion.

Tophet shook her head so hard her long platinum hair swished around her arms and waist. "I can't. It's awful. I just can't tell you."

At long last, Death stepped forward. "I can."

Tophet startled. "Oh, dog's breath!"

"What's the matter, Toffee, baby? Too much public humiliation for one day? I heard you trying to blame it all on me. Let's bring back that book, shall we?"

Tophet looked at the sky. "Look, I'm sorry I sleazed out of taking responsibility for it, but..." She shrugged.

Death strolled up to Blaze and Heather. "See? There's justice in the world. Maybe not in your world. Not yet. But down here, with my lovely woman in charge, never fear. Her logic and reason are bound to straighten things out—eventually. Meanwhile, if she keeps making these monumental blunders, the world will keep right on rolling toward certain doom."

Tophet whirled away from him and slapped her hands over her ears. "La, la, la, la, la, la..."

Death shook his head, raised his volume, and talked over the noise. "See what I mean? Scary, huh? And she's in charge."

CHAPTER TWENTY

Death poofed the mortals off to an unoccupied lecture hall. This time he didn't bother to change out of his black robe. Standing at the podium, he cleared his throat. "Students, this is important information you should have in case—I mean, *when* you get back to your own world.

"There are three categories of suicides. One is for those who give their lives for the good of others. Heroes. Another is for those who kill themselves to avoid a prolonged, painful death or a life that's worse than death. Dr. Kevorkian-style."

Death paused for effect. He rolled up his long, loose sleeves and then focused on the mortals. "The third group is the one Tophet didn't want to talk about." He snapped his fingers and suddenly the couple each held a notebook and pen. "Write this down. She's probably not too proud of what she did with the third group, but to blame it on me?" He shook his head and stalked across the stage. "Well, that's just wrong. This is a misunderstanding I have to straighten out."

"Talk slow," Blaze said. "I want to get this all down."

"And so you should! There's no difference in the way the first two groups are recycled, or reincarnated as you say. It's as if they died a natural death. But the third group... Well, the third group is made up of people who killed themselves in order to harm others. Suicide bombers, pilots who deliberately crash into populated areas and the like. This group also includes people who take the lives of others and then don't stick around to discuss it."

Heather raised her hand. "What's to discuss?"

"The trial. Sometimes people refer to them as evil. I don't know if they are or not. One example you've heard of is currently out in the pond with an experimental group. You know his name. It begins with H."

"How do you spell deliberately?" Blaze asked.

Heather whispered to him and pointed to her paper.

"That's right, Mortal Number Two. Let him copy from your paper. There won't be a test on this material, but it's vitally important to get it now because I won't be repeating myself."

Blaze looked at Heather's paper and frantically scribbled.

"This group, students, gets stuck in a loop. Tophet thought it was obvious they hadn't learned the non-destructivity lesson, so she decided to bring them back right away. No rest for the wicked, so to speak."

Heather was listening with rapt attention and Blaze was writing down every word.

"Do any of you see a problem with that?"

Blaze and Heather looked at each other, shrugged and then shook their heads.

"Remember how groups of people tend to come back together?"

They nodded but still looked confused.

"Think, people. It's obvious. She brings a prematurely ejected soul back into the same family as soon as possible to try again. How many of you would want your kids to be your parents? Or maybe, if you're still young, you could have the same parents but be your brothers' and sisters' younger sibling."

Blaze groaned and slapped his forehead. "Shit, I tortured my little brothers!"

Heather gasped and grabbed her throat. "What about those who are the only child of a single mother?"

Death shrugged. "Adoption or maybe your maiden Aunty gets married and pregnant. Tophet finds a way to get you back into the same gene pool, to be as closely related to yourself as possible."

Heather raised her hand.

"Yes, Mortal Number Two?"

"How can that possibly help the suicide rate?"

Death crossed his arms. "It doesn't. It doesn't help the problem at all. In fact, it can make it worse. Yeah, she really botched that one. So far there seems to be only one solution, but as she said, it isn't pretty."

"What is it?" Blaze and Heather asked in unison.

"Come with me and I'll show you." One lightning bolt later, they were back at the pond.

***

Tophet was still facing away with her hands over her ears when they returned. Heather noticed time had a funny way of moving in the shifts. Minutes could pass in seconds. She wondered if Tophet knew they had been gone.

Death pointed to the pond and began explaining. "She has decided to send them back to square one. The primordial ooze stage. The soul in question must start all over again. You can see a few of them floating on top as algae. Pond scum."

"Eww," Heather said. "And you had nothing to do with this?"

"Me? You must be kidding. Her mistakes are complicating the world of mortals and increasing my workload." Death clasped his hands behind his back and paced in a circle. "It could be an effective deterrent if people knew their options were to return as their own descendant or as pond scum. But nobody knows this. If we could just get the word out, maybe your warped world would have a chance to turn around in your lifetime."

Tophet whirled around and removed her hands from her ears. "Oh yeah?"

Death stared her down. "Nice comeback, but a little late. I'd stay and play 'Confession is good for the soul', but I have a quota to satisfy. If I don't meet it, I may have to ignore the order and grab whatever souls are handy."

"No, don't do that," Blaze pleaded. "I don't want to be related to myself!"

Death gave him a blank stare before he disappeared. Heather slipped her arm around Blaze and patted his back.

Tophet jammed her hands on her hips. "Oh, calm down. I won't let him take you. Even if he did, I'd deem it an accident and the worst that could happen would be a career in the insurance industry."

"Oh no!" Heather had fleetingly entertained the thought of hanging herself from the nearest tree even on a good day at Phoenix Insurance.

"Look, there's no more time for questions or melodrama, Mortals One and Two. I need to get you back to your lives before midnight. It's dusk now and obviously I'm not going to get any help from Mr. Reaper."

Blaze shook his head. "Now I know why they call him 'Grim'."

Death's voice resonated from the sky. "Watch what you say, people."

Tophet yelled back, "They've got lives, you know! I could use some help to get the mortals back to them."

She dropped into a chair and rested her chin on her fist in a pose that resembled *The Thinker*. "Forget him," she said. "I'm a great believer in destiny, despite some of my callous remarks. I have to believe that your coming here is part of Fate's plan."

Blaze sat crossed legged on the grass. "I don't get it."

"Don't you see? When things aren't happening as expected, it's sometimes Fate taking control. Of course, sometimes it's your own fool-headed, stubborn self-will."

Blaze scratched his head. "Like when all your relationships don't work out until you meet the right one; or losing a job makes it possible to get a better job?"

"Exactly. At the time it seems to make no sense but then later..."

"Are you saying this experience could lead to a better next life?"

Tophet clapped her hands. "That's it! All you have to do to fulfill your destiny is figure out what Fate is trying to tell you and cooperate."

"Oh, is that all?" Blaze rolled his eyes.

Heather noticed a round shimmer behind Tophet. It appeared to be growing larger. As it took shape and cleared, she recognized the familiar round face and kind blue eyes of the Moon Goddess.

"Goddess!" Heather and Blaze exclaimed.

Tophet whirled around. "Oh, Gods."

The Moon Goddess, robed in her shining blue-white gown, opened her arms, and beamed. "Relax, Tophet. I'm here on an errand of mercy."

Tophet looked shocked. "Mercy? For me? I don't know what to say."

"No, you never do."

She pushed past her toward Blaze and Heather. "The mercy isn't for you. It's for these poor unfortunate mortals who are depending upon you." She faced Tophet and set a hand on their shoulders. "The sun has set. Did you notice how the light is fading?"

Tophet folded her arms. "Is that what you came to tell me? What time it is?"

"I shouldn't have to. I actually came for two reasons. I wanted to see them one more time and to find out why the word destiny is coming up so often."

Heather hugged her around the waist. "You could hear our conversations?"

"Well, it's a little harder now that she's installed the sound barrier." The Goddess glared at Tophet. "But I can get the gist."

"The mortals were wondering about their destinies. Is that any of your business, eavesdropper?" Tophet looked down her nose at the Goddess.

The Goddess scowled, then took a deep breath and stepped away from the mortal couple toward Tophet. "You know, Tophet, I don't have anything against you. I just don't think you fully understand the concept of..." The Goddess raised her glowing arms to the sky with an awestruck expression. "Destiny!" Her voice echoed.

"Look, Goddess, destiny really isn't so furtive or mystifying. I would think you'd realize because of the work I do, I'd know a little bit about it."

The Goddess shook her finger at Tophet. "You may think you know all about destiny and when it comes to the destiny of a soul's next life, you're the expert. But there's so much more to..." Again, she raised her arms toward the sky and beamed. "Destiny!" This time her melodic voice seemed louder and echoed longer. She sighed and a satisfied smile crossed her bright face. In a clear soprano, she sang.

In the quiet hours of reflection
I learned to thank you for rejection.
Without your gift of peace and time,
I wouldn't know what role was mine,
and I'm important, as you'll see
in what you treat as destiny.

Tophet paced back and forth; her brow furrowed. "If there's a point to this, I wish you'd hurry up and get to it. Otherwise, you may as well go stick your nose in one of your craters and go back to meditating on the fate of the universe, or whatever nonsense you're referring to. Let me worry about the fates of these two souls."

The Goddess bunched her hands into fists and hummed. Then she sang louder than before.

"I learned to like aloneness,
even with all my croneness.
I sat by the fire and ate,
and didn't watch my weight,

and wished you well with all your skin and boneness!

I know you didn't learn at all,
and off I go to watch you fall.
I will not laugh or wish you ill,
or try to freeze you with my chill,
because that's what you'd do, my friend,
and that's why you'll fail in the end.

With all your focused energy
on mortal lives and not on me
you'd live life as a joyous dance,
instead of in a numbing trance.
Now off I go to hang with stars,
and you can just go straight to Mars.

The Goddess turned three quarters of the way around and rose into the sky. Before long a glowing gibbous moon played hide and seek behind the clouds.

"Wait!" Heather cried.

Blaze set his hands on his hips and shook his head. "Nice going, Toph'."

"Don't listen to her! We don't need that self-righteous, haughty, pretentious..." Tophet shook her fist at the moon. "Errr!"

"You lookin' for a word, Tophet?" Blaze asked.

"Yeah, what have ya got?"

"Nothing. I can think of a few to describe you though, Bone-head."

Deep red showed on Tophet's face even in the fading light. She clenched her fists and shook violently. At last, she exploded in a bellow. "Death!"

Blaze blanched. Heather could feel her throat constrict.

"We're sorry. Please don't bother him. We'll be good," Heather said. "I just thought she might be able to—"

Death flashed in as a bolt of lightning and wedged himself between Tophet and the mortals. "Don't say another word," he commanded. "Tophet, you and I need to talk."

"What about them?" she asked, pointing to Blaze and Heather.

"What do you mean?"

"Aren't you going to talk to them? Don't they need to be told to respect their elders?"

"Who do you think I am? Some 1950's TV father?" He turned to the couple and wagged a finger at them. "Kids, you know better than to talk to your immortal that way. Now say you're sorry."

"We already did," Blaze explained.

Death let out a deep breath and turned to Tophet. "So, what do you want, a firing squad? Look, he was right. You can be a bonehead sometimes. Let's send them to the Goddess for a while and discuss this rationally."

"She can keep them for all I care. Do you have any idea how hard it is to be stuck at home with a couple of little mortals driving me crazy all day?"

"No, she can't keep them." Death put an arm around her. "They came to you. Weren't you just talking about destiny? Don't you realize they're here, with you, for a reason?"

Tophet glared at the couple. "It would serve them right. All of them." She heaved a sigh and hesitated. "Fine. Let her babysit for a while and then we'll see how mellow and spiritual she is. But you and I really do need to talk about how to get rid of them—I mean, send them back—while they're gone."

"Fine," Death said.

"Fine," Blaze and Heather echoed.

Tophet materialized her spoon, pointed it at the mortals, said "Fine!" and poof, they were gone.

CHAPTER TWENTY-ONE

Tophet's shoulders drooped and she laid her palm across her forehead. "Thanks for coming. I was getting to the point of desperation."

"So where do I come in?" Death crossed his arms.

"I don't know. How about if you hang out with me so I don't have to drink alone?"

"That's not going to solve our dilemma. We need clear heads more than anything, now."

"I know." Resigned, she materialized a couch underneath her, sank onto it and burst into tears.

"Baby, don't. You know I can't stand to see you cry." Death sat beside her and cradled her in his arms. "We'll figure this out. You're just tired and upset. Try to relax. We'll come up with something before midnight."

Tophet blubbered, sniffed, and then slowly pulled herself together. She picked up a corner of Death's loose sleeve and blew her nose on it.

"Toffee, that's..."

She looked into his eyes through fresh, brimming tears.

"Never mind." He held her against his hard, muscled chest. Using his other sleeve, he dried her eyes. She had to admit, but only to herself, that his gesture touched her deeply.

"I guess you do care," she whispered.

"Of course, I do, baby. How could you doubt that?"

"The Goddess..."

"Oh no. Not again."

Tophet tried to pull away from him, but he held on tight.

"She was nothing to me. *Is* nothing to me. If you would just remember that and find a way to get over your jealousy..."

"I don't know if I can. Even as a crone she's beautiful. And she's got the beauty inside too. I'm a wretched, self-centered, overly critical, immature bitch. Inside and out."

Death smiled. "But that's what I love about you, baby. I can't handle all that serenity and sensitivity crap." Death cupped his hand behind her head and pulled her toward his mouth. He nibbled her lower lip. On a sigh she opened to him, and he slid his tongue inside. Death gave her the longest, most passionate kiss the two of them had shared in centuries.

When they reluctantly separated, he murmured, "Sweetheart?"

Tophet could hardly believe her ears. Had he just called her sweetheart and hinted that he loved her? She stared at him without blinking.

"Sweetheart, would you feel better if we fucked?"

Precious moment over.

Tophet smirked. "If I had any inclinations toward sentimentality, that proposition might have been a crushing disappointment. Thankfully I'm more comfortable with raw honesty than poetry."

"So, is that a yes?"

Tophet let her actions speak for her. She reclined on the couch and poofed off her robe. Death looked as if he were a starving dog eyeing a juicy steak. She let her knees open and close in a gentle teasing wave.

Death whipped off his clothing, including his black boxer-briefs and leaned over her. His enormous cock jutted out. "Want to play with my joystick?"

"I thought you wanted to pleasure me?"

"Absolutely, baby. How about some sixty-nine action?"

"1969? With psychedelics or something?"

Death rolled his eyes. "You're just pretending to misunderstand me, aren't you?"

"I couldn't help myself." She grinned. "This couch isn't really suited to the sixty-nine position."

Death spread his robe over the grass as if a gentleman covering a puddle for a delicate lady to step on, and then extended his hand. She took it, then gazed into his eyes, and rose regally from the couch.

"I'm gonna suck you good, baby," he said.

Tophet smiled and assumed the bottom position, waiting for Death to kneel by her shoulders. He leaned over her torso and began licking.

"Ohh..."

His cock was pointed at her mouth like a compass, and she knew just what she was going to do. She started off by teasing it with her tongue. A few licks here, a few laps there. Torturing him, sexually, would make her feel better if nothing else did.

A quiver radiated from her clit as he brushed it with his tongue. She figured she had to give in order to get, so she took just the head of his cock into her mouth and withdrew, giving it a gentle suck as she pulled back. For that she earned a lick and a nibble.

Okay, I see what he's up to. She took his length into her mouth and rolled her tongue around it as she once again pulled back. He lapped her clit a few more times. She arched her back and moaned around his cock. She sucked on him like a tootsie pop, a little harder and longer.

He took her clit into his mouth, sucking and licking until she couldn't deal with his satin-wrapped steel rod practically poking out the back of her esophagus anymore. Using her hand to keep up the pressure on his moistened cock, she licked his balls furiously. He focused all of his attention on her sensitive nub, and she trembled all over with building ecstasy.

Unable to hold back her unintelligible words, which were beginning to sound like her tongue was stuck to a frozen flagpole, she stopped licking and just held on for the ride. Vibrating and quivering like a volcano ready to erupt, she let the rippling pleasure overtake her. Waves of pure ecstasy crashed in on her and radiated outward throughout her entire body. She screamed in bliss as her climax rocked her body, spreading its soothing fingers from her core to her hair follicles.

"Ahh..." she sighed and panted.

Death rolled off to the side, swiped the back of his hand across his glistening mouth and smiled at her. "I've still got it baby. Right?"

"Yes. Nicely done."

"So, how do you want to do me?"

Tophet gave him a weak smile. "You mean when, don't you?"

"Aw, c'mon baby. I did you, now it's your turn to do me. If you're going to poop out on me after a really big 'O' then maybe I shouldn't be so skillful."

"Sorry. Can't move. How about if you hover?"

Death frowned. "What do you think I am? A friggin' heli-copter? I'd probably lose control during my orgasm and crash land on your face."

Tophet chuckled. After a couple more deep breaths she struggled to push herself up on her elbows. "I was only kidding. Where do you want me?"

"Why don't you just lie there and let me do all the work?"

"Really? Thanks." Tophet let her elbows collapse under her and she returned to her sunny side up position.

Death stood up and leaned over her. "That time, I was kid-ding."

"Oh."

He raked a hand through his hair and looked at the sky. "You know, the mortals have been gone a while. We should probably bring them back. I'll take a rain check on that orgasm, but only if you promise to make up for it."

Tophet stood on shaky legs and poofed her robe on. "I promise."

"That's my girl." He kissed her on top of her head and then he picked up his robe. It was wrinkled and stained so he poofed it into oblivion. In a flash he had a brand new one. "So who do you think should go after them?"

She looked at him, folding her arms. "Neither one of us. We can send for them, but you knew that."

"Oh, good idea," Death said.

Tophet eyed him with suspicion.

"What?"

"Looking for an excuse to see someone?"

His eyes narrowed. "I don't need an excuse. If I wanted to go, I'd go."

She shrugged. "True. Well, I'm going to send for them anyway."

"You do that."

Her long, metal spoon materialized in her hand, and she scooped the sky with it. "Come here, mortals—through the portals." She looked at Death and shrugged. "It was the best I could do on short notice."

A moment and a puff of smoke later, Blaze appeared.

He looked around and stated the obvious. "Oops. No Heather."

Tophet's face flushed and she found it difficult to keep the aggravation out of her voice. "Where was she when you last saw her?"

Blaze shrugged. "She was sitting on a crater talking to the Goddess. I was off exploring. I wish I'd had a confederate flag to leave with my footprints. That would've been so cool."

Tophet slapped both hands over her mouth, hard, as if to hold in a scream.

"I'll get her," Death said. He disappeared in a flash and returned with a recalcitrant Heather.

Tophet exploded. "What is your problem, young lady?"

Heather opened her mouth to speak, but before she could, Tophet held up her hand. "No. I don't want to hear it. I'm really fed up with you for not coming when you're called."

"But..." Heather's face showed a look of desperation.

"Zip it!" Tophet shouted.

Heather's mouth closed from one side to the other, as if an invisible zipper had been pulled across her face. She made some muffled sounds and Blaze grabbed her by both her shoulders.

"Heather?"

She shook her head, unable to speak.

Blaze glared at Tophet. "What did you do?"

Death rolled his eyes. "I'm out of here." In a flash he was gone, leaving Tophet to deal with the furious mortals alone.

CHAPTER TWENTY-TWO

After unzipping Heather's mouth, Tophet watched as Blaze and Heather stormed off into the dark woods leaving her to think things over. What was their problem? Did everyone prefer the ugly, barren moon to this lush and colorful environment?

Tophet looked over at the shimmering glow of the pond at night. It really was quite beautiful. The blue of the water mixed with the glow of the green souls lit up the area with its brilliant iridescence. She heaved a deep sigh. She knew it wasn't the place they objected to; it was the person. The immortal in charge.

"Why am I such a jerk?" Tophet paced, head hung, and a tear slipped down her cheek. "I try to be nice. I really do try. I think I'm doing fine with them and the next thing I know, they push my buttons and I fly off the handle."

She plunked her body down. A rock appeared but being a little off center, Tophet rolled off and fell on the ground.

"Damn it!" She got up, brushed the grass off and rubbed her sore hip. "I've had nothing but problems today. It hasn't been boring, but honest to Pete Moss..."

Heather and Blaze emerged from the woods holding hands. Although they looked hesitant, they approached the pouting immortal, anyway.

Blaze cleared his throat. "I'm sorry for yelling at you."

"Oh. An apology?" She hadn't known what to expect, but it certainly wasn't that. Tophet didn't know what to do. "I...I guess you're forgiven. I mean...um, don't do it again."

"I'll try not to. We have important things to discuss, and all this fighting is just wasting time."

"You're right, Mortal Number One. So, what have you come up with?"

"Me? I thought you and Death were going to figure something out."

"Well, ah... We... I guess there's one thing we know for sure."

"What's that?"

"Well, whoever said it—I can't remember now—came up with a great idea. You two can be my mortal messengers. I need to communicate the fate of the world to those who would destroy it and each other. The problems in the Earthly realm would undoubtedly lessen if people only knew the long-range consequences of their behavior."

"So how do we do that?" Blaze asked.

"All I have to do is make sure you get back with some kind of memory implanted to be triggered at the proper time."

"An implant? Like chips in our necks?"

They both took a giant step backward.

"No, nothing that drastic."

Blaze shrugged. "Why don't you just tell us what you want us to say, and we'll remember?"

"It's not that simple."

Tophet paced back and forth with her hands clasped behind her back. "I still haven't figured out a way to get you back there yet. I also need to wipe your memory of your time spent here; you're not supposed to know this realm exists."

Heather timidly raised her hand.

"Not now, Mortal Number Two, I'm trying to concentrate."

"Fine," Blaze said. "We'll take some kind of message with us and do what we're supposed to do, but how the hell are we going to pull this off?"

"Which part?"

"Either part. Any part. It seems like we need a miracle to get us out of here and another one to remember something you want us to say."

"I can give you the message through hypnosis," Tophet said. "I'll have to think of the very simplest form of that message though, and use a word or phrase to trigger the stored knowledge."

Blaze threw his hands in the air. "That's just great. We'll be here for centuries. You can't even come up with one foul-mouthed curse-word!"

"Oh, for crying out loud," she snapped. Remembering how her reactions put people off, she took 10 deep breaths and tried to stay calm. "I can too. I just enjoy the challenge. How would you deal with the loneliness? The tedium? The isolation?"

Blaze shrugged. "I'd open a club."

"What kind of club?" she asked.

He stroked his chin as he thought out loud. "I don't know. Every club needs some sort of gimmick. Maybe since I had a past life in China where I was all wise, it could be like an Asian Palace."

Tophet raised her eyebrows. "You mean like the emperor's palace in which you lived?"

"Yeah, Geisha waitresses!"

"I'm sorry to disappoint you Mortal Number One, but Geishas are part of the Japanese culture, and they don't like it when people get them mixed up."

"Okay, so we'll have bite-size Chinese food instead of pretzels. And a happy hour with discounted umbrella drinks...but the music has to be rock." Excited, he babbled on and mimicked Tophet's habit of pacing. "We can have a DJ and a big dance floor in the beginning; we'll get live bands later on when we become more popular. Of course, I'll book my own band whenever I want..."

"Hold on, cowboy." With a wave of her magic spoon, she created an enormous palace based on his description and brought the club to life.

"Yeah, that's it! This is cool."

They all stood at the entrance, Heather, and Blaze gawking inside. People were dancing to the rock music the DJ played. The bar hosted several patrons sipping umbrella drinks and snacking on bite-sized egg rolls and sesame sticks. Couples danced and laughed.

"It's exactly how I imagined it," Blaze exclaimed.

"Yes, I know." Tophet crossed her arms, looking pleased with herself.

"Did you read my mind again?"

"No, I didn't have to. You just jabbered out the whole plan. I simply modeled it after the palace where you used to live."

"Wow." Awed, Blaze looked all around, taking in the majestic view.

"Can we go in?"

"Sure," Tophet said. "But keep in mind, no one can see you. You're quite invisible."

"Damn, every time I think we're back among Earthlings, it turns out we're invisible. Is there anything you can do to fix that?"

Tophet sighed. "You're in another dimension not on another planet, Mortal Number One. She closed her eyes and rested a finger on her chin as she was thinking. "I'm not sure. I may be able to do something temporary."

"Can you try it? I need to party, and I'd also like to take Heather out on a proper date. That is, if she'll go out with me?"

Heather's eyes sparkled as she nodded enthusiastically.

Tophet pulled her spoon from nothing but air. "Okay but remember it's only temporary. And no fairy Godmother jokes!"

"None," Blaze promised and crossed his heart.

Tophet's spoon held something that looked like glitter and she threw it over their heads.

A couple exited the building and almost bumped into them.

"Oh, excuse me," said the woman.

"You can see us?" Blaze asked, excitedly.

The woman turned around after she passed them and gave him a strange look, as if to say, of course I can, you idiot. Blaze couldn't have been more excited. He held out his hand to Heather, and she wove her fingers through his, giving him a squeeze and a smile.

"You can't stay long," Tophet reminded them.

Blaze grinned. "We know. When's pumpkin time?"

Her eyes narrowed. "I thought I just said—"

"Oh yeah. No fairy Godmother jokes. Sorry about that."

"Go on. Everything you could possibly want is inside. I need some time to think about our mission."

He pulled Heather behind him and strutted into the palatial building.

Lucky mortals. It only takes the tiniest distraction to amuse them.

CHAPTER TWENTY-THREE

Tophet sighed and sat on the steps. "Alone at last."

Death popped into her field of vision.

She glanced up at him. "Oh, rot."

"Fine, I can tell when I'm not wanted." He raised his robed arms as if to disappear.

"Wait!"

He stopped and looked at her curiously.

"I'm sorry, Death. I've been surrounded by the castaways for a little too long. And to think...I used to wish I weren't so alone."

Death sat down beside her on the steps. "I didn't realize you minded the loneliness." He slipped his arm around her back. "I'll have to spend more time with you after they leave."

"You would have anyway. I'm boffing you." She rested her head on his shoulder. Her sleeve extended a few feet beyond her body along the step. A couple of mortal girls ran up the stairs until one of them tripped over the invisible material and almost fell.

"Oops, careful of that step."

"What did you trip over?" the other girl asked.

The first girl shrugged. "I don't know. My own feet, I guess."

Tophet snickered and elbowed Death. "Does that happen to you?"

"Yeah. Sometimes I do it on purpose. What else do you think that useless scythe is for?"

They chuckled and then fell into a comfortable silence. Death stroked her arm again. "I have to admit that sometimes I'm not happy about the need to operate undercover so much. There are only so many mortals you can trip before you wish you could show yourself."

"Are you saying you get lonely too?"

"Sure, I do. Don't you feel differently with the kids around? More—I don't know—complete?"

"No, but I do feel more harried and inconvenienced. I wonder if that's what parenthood feels like?" Tophet asked.

"Probably. Makes you feel sorry for breeders, doesn't it?"

"Yeah, but sometimes the way Mortals Number One and Number Two look to me for guidance, or bitch at me, or shake in their shoes when they piss me off is enthralling. Sometimes they treat us as if we're no different from humans. But we are different. I feel it more acutely now than ever before." Tophet fluffed her brown robe out on the steps around her and clasped her hands around her knees.

"I know what you mean," Death said.

"So how do you deal with it?"

"Well, I wasn't going to tell you, but since you seem to understand now..." He kicked at the step and hesitated. "That's how that thing happened with the Moon Goddess. I was just trying to fill the loneliness of being without you."

Tophet jumped up. "You had to bring that up, didn't you? And now you're trying to make it sound like I should feel sorry for you and take the blame."

"Toffee, please. You were rejecting my attentions."

She threw her hands in the air. "I would have caved, if only you had been a little more persistent and a lot more romantic."

"But—"

"No!" She said and jammed her hands on her hips. "I should have seen it coming. After all, you've always been partial to older women."

Death tapped his foot. "Look, are you going to calm down or do I have to distract you by starting a fire in this club? Then we'll both have to get back to work, or maybe I should just toss you over my knee and..."

"Don't burn down the palace, Mortals Number One and Two are in there!"

Death shook his head. "A few hours ago, you wanted me to take them out and shoot them."

"I know, I know. But now I think we can use them to correct a grave error."

He perked up. "My favorite kind. You did say 'we', didn't you? Does that mean our deal is still on? We can fuck again?"

"I'm going to get over it, eventually."

He blew out a deep breath. "Good. It would be a shame to lose the lo—I mean, the chemistry that's happening between us."

"Oh, cut it out, Death. I know how you feel, and I don't want to lose it either. You have a decent side and it's really quite charming."

He smirked. "If you tell anyone, I'll deny it. What tipped you off?"

"You've expressed so much concern for my charges."

"What you spend is none of my business."

"Death, you know what I'm talking about. The mortals."

He smiled. "I've come to know them, and I can't help but respect the way they're handling all of this. How did you know it wasn't all because of you?"

"Because you wouldn't let me do anything foolish with them. Ordinarily you wouldn't have cared about that."

"Well, I do have to get going, Toffee, baby. Please, don't make any mistakes with them while I'm gone."

"I wasn't planning on it." She frowned and folded her arms.

"Yeah, well you never do."

"You're as bad as Mortal Number One, saying whatever pops into your head to whomever you please with no regard as to how it might be taken."

"At least we're both honest. I'll drop in from time to time in case you need me." Death raised his arms.

"Actually, I could use some help with—"

He disappeared in a poof.

"Or not…"

CHAPTER TWENTY-FOUR

A few minutes later, Tophet was standing next to the side of the building, butting her head against the wall, muttering to herself the entire time.

"Hypnotize them first and then send them back with a post-hypnotic suggestion. But what should it be?"

She straightened up and rubbed her forehead. "Oh...I'm so bad at picking the right words." She staggered to the stairs and slowly lowered herself onto them. "Let's see. The concept of religion didn't frighten them into behaving themselves. I could tell them to reason with people." She snorted. "Yeah, right. Like humans would take diplomacy more seriously. They can't even be diplomatic about differences in religions."

She beat her head with her fists. "Think!"

The door to the club flew open and she turned around to watch a big brute toss two squirming male patrons out onto the steps, yelling, "And stay out!"

One patron eyed the other one angrily and growled, "You ass-wipe, she wasn't lookin' at you."

The other guy yelled, "What are you? Brain dead? I could have gotten lucky tonight, but you screwed it up for me you snot-rag."

Tophet stood, her eyebrows raised, hoping they'd trade a few more insults. Maybe something she could use?

"Puke face."

"Low life."

"Freak."

"Asshole."

They seemed to be slowing down to a simmer when she decided to throw some sparkling dust over herself—and maybe some fuel on the fire. Materializing unnoticed, she approached them from the bottom of the steps. "Please continue."

They looked at each other for a moment and then back at Tophet.

"What are you lookin' at?" one of them said.

The other one eyed her suspiciously. "You want us to fight?"

"Sure," she said. "I'm interested in your technique. You seem to know how to blow off steam."

"That's one for the books," the first guy said.

"Yeah. She must be some kind of psychology researcher or something."

"Research this!" one of them said as he raised his middle finger. The guys laughed and slapped each other on their backs.

Heather and Blaze stepped out of the club and Heather pointed at the two guys. "That's them," she said.

The first guy turned around, saw them, and puffed out his chest. "There you are, little Miss Prick Tease."

The other one ran up the steps toward her. Blaze stepped between them but before the inevitable meeting, a flash of lightning split the air between the two young men. An angry Death appeared in all his black-hooded glory.

The guy running at Blaze fell to his knees. "Oh my God! Hail Mary, full of grace…"

"My name ain't Mary," Death said. "But your name is mud if you touch this girl. Now stuff the wounded pride and step away from the beauty queen."

Both young strangers were frozen in fear. A moment later, they both disappeared in a puff of smoke.

Heather gasped. "What did you? Where did you send them?"

"It wasn't him," Tophet said. "It was me, and yes, they're safe. At least until they give in to their own stupidity again."

"I didn't think you could be seen here," Blaze said.

Tophet shrugged. "I never tried."

Death shook his head. "She can and she knows she can. She just chooses not to. And she's right. We're not supposed to."

Tophet gestured to the spot where the angry men had once stood. A yellow puddle dripped from one step to the step below. "See what happens when we show up? That's the least of the fallout."

"I wouldn't have had to materialize at all if you hadn't created yet another dimension in which to stir up trouble."

"Oh, knock it off, Death. You sound like I do this every day when in fact I've never done it before."

Blaze cocked his head to the side. "You said you had to remain hidden. That's like one of the first things you said to us."

"Can you blame me for avoidance? Look at the idiots populating other dimensions."

Blaze folded his arms. "We're not all idiots. You've even found you could like a couple of us."

Tophet laughed. "What makes you think that?"

"By the way you've been looking out for us. If you didn't like us, you'd have left us to get lost in the forest, or you'd have drowned us in the pond."

"Don't give me ideas."

Death put an arm around her waist. "He's right, you know. You pretend you can't stand them, but you just do that to keep from being hurt. I've done the same thing lots of times." He lowered his voice so only she could hear him. "We've done that with each other."

Tophet folded her arms and turned up her nose. "I was bored, and I found the mortals to be entertaining, so I tolerated them."

Blaze chuckled. "Yeah, right. Like when Heather and I were making love. You finally had lots of time to yourself, but what did you do? You spied on us."

Tophet raised her eyebrows. "You knew?"

"Well, yeah, but there wasn't much we could do about it. You probably picked up a few tips. You and Death seem like you're doing a little better."

"What? How dare—?"

"It's true, Toffee, baby. I like the kinky new you." Death shrugged. "At least, I like how you're into me."

"Well, look, I hate to change the subject, but it's getting late. We've wasted a lot of time with this sharing and caring crap. Now let's get back to the pond and get you home—if we can."

CHAPTER TWENTY-FIVE

Blaze and Heather sat cross-legged on the grass. Their only light was the eerie illumination emanating from the pond of souls. They concentrated on the pocket-watch Tophet dangled and swung in front of them.

"Feel your eyelids getting heavy. Heavy. Heavier. Heavier and heavier. You're completely relaxed. You're almost asleep."

Death strolled in, startling her. "That's what I love about you time-honored traditionalists. You know there's a better way, but you keep going back to the same old thing."

"Shh!" Tophet stuffed the watch into her robe. "What better way?"

Death snickered. "Watch this."

Tophet heard faint music in the background. It was strangely reminiscent of something she couldn't quite put a name to and then it hit her. Oh, for the love of James T. Kirk. It's the stupid Star Trek theme.

Death crossed to the space between the mortals and placed his hand on Blaze's shoulder. Delivering a firm pinch, Blaze yawned, lay down in the grass and fell asleep.

Death repeated the process with Heather. She curled up next to Blaze and lay motionless. Both were breathing the long, slow breaths of a deep sleep.

"Where did you learn that?"

"Moments after he died, Gene Roddenberry showed me how to do it. Hey, is he still out there?" Death nodded toward the pond.

"No, I sent him back years ago. As soon as he grows up, he's going to completely restructure NASA. Ironically, his parents are big fans of his old stuff, but he prefers George Lucas."

"I'll drink to irony." Death reached into his black cape and pulled out a Brandy Sling and Bloody Mary. Handing the Brandy to Tophet, he raised his glass. "Here's to finally getting those kids home so we can fool around as much as we want."

Tophet grinned and clinked his glass. "Nice of you to remember my poison."

Death smiled and raised his glass again to the sleeping mortals. "To sweet dreams and haunting memories."

"What kind of haunting memories do you think they'll have?"

Death winked. "The kind they'll talk about for years."

Tophet slipped her arm around Death's waist. They drained their glasses and tossed them over their shoulders. Instead of falling to the ground, they disappeared in mid-air.

Tophet hummed and Death picked up the melody, chanting the words in a deep melodic voice.

Dream sweet dreams,
but remember one.
You had it
for a reason.

Tophet took over and sang in her breathy alto.

Your destiny seems to
be in the sun,
and I'll try to make
it pleasin'.

Death raised his eyebrows and smirked. She shrugged and continued.

You'll have to be famous,
to reach the masses
and we'll be watching,
with special glasses.

Tophet faded into her harmonizing hum and let Death finish the song.

Since you'll have partial memory,
you must remember this dream for me,
and tell the world the vision you see.
Now what is it, can you tell me?

Without opening his eyes, Blaze said in a sleepy voice, "Death is serious business. It should be left to the professional."

"And..." Heather added, "Suicide sucks."

Hmm, you're getting close,
but what I want the most
is to hear you say
what I taught you today.

The sleeping couple chanted in unison.

That no one's right and no one's wrong,
if different voices sing the song.
Combining all our mortal talents,
Together, we'll restore the balance.

The 'powers that be'
watch our actions
but do not favor
any factions.

They'll leave our fates
in our own hands.
We must stop hate
and save the lands...

Death let out a deep breath. "I knew they were listening on some level, even if it was subconscious. I think they've got it now."

Tophet sighed. "Look at them. Sweet smiles on their faces, sleeping so peacefully."

"Yeah... So, do you want to give them their trigger word or words now?"

"Yes. I finally came up with something appropriate that I know they'll hear—a lot." She bent over them and whispered, "World Peace."

Death nodded his approval.

"It all seems to be going perfectly, so far. Of course, we still don't know how to send them back." She began to pace. "I don't suppose you found out anything?"

Death fell into step beside her. "Actually, I did. I found out there's another immortal who knows the answer, but I don't know who it is."

Heather, still asleep, raised her hand. The immortals paced right by her. She waved and eventually grunted.

"Not now, Mortal Number Two. Time's growing short. You should have gone to the bathroom before we put you into stasis."

Death stared at Heather, whose hand remained fixed in the air. "Wait, I think she's trying to tell us she knows the answer."

Heather sat up and opened her eyes, nodding furiously.

"Well, speak!" Tophet demanded.

She blew out a deep breath. A look of relief softened the creases on her forehead and around her hope-filled eyes. "The Moon Goddess knows. That's why I was late getting back. I was asking her about it, and I think she was about to tell me the answer."

Death jammed his hands on his hips. "Shit."

"Why the hell didn't you tell us?" Tophet screeched.

"Because you told me not to speak unless specifically asked to."

Death crossed his robed arms and frowned at Tophet. "Brilliant."

Heather yawned and curled up in Blaze's arms.

Tophet's pinched face relaxed. "Look, there's no time for blame and ridicule. It's getting late. One of us should go to the Goddess, and since you were the one having a 'thing' with her..."

"Are you going to hold that over my head for the rest of eternity?"

"No, but I'm sure she doesn't want to talk to me. Besides, I'd probably taunt her."

"Look, I told you it was off and on. As of now and as long as you're with me, baby, it's off with her. Way off."

"Then maybe you should take this opportunity to make nice and just be friends?"

He narrowed his eyes at Tophet, loomed large and then disappeared in a crash of thunder and a bolt of lightning.

"I hate it when he does that."

Tophet looked down and noticed Heather was still awake. "I'm glad you're awake, Mortal Number Two. I feel I should apologize. I didn't mean to get so angry. It's just you scared the daylights out of me."

"That's okay. You kind of reminded me of my mom when you did that."

Tophet sat beside her. "Really? I thought you didn't like your mom?"

"I love my mom."

Tophet smiled and patted her on the head. "You'd better get some sleep, so you can forget this place really exists and just think of it as a dream."

"I wish I didn't have to forget," Heather said.

Tophet pulled her pocket watch out of her robe. "Tell you what, when I send you back, I'll grant you one special wish. That will make up for our misunderstanding and thank you for giving us the last clue to this puzzle."

"Really? Can you do that?"

"I can alter fate a bit. Of course, it's up to you to live life to the fullest after that."

"How about Blaze? He was pretty upset about the whole misunderstanding and only kept his mouth shut because I asked him to."

"Okay, then. Blaze will get something he wants too.

"Will you know what we want?"

"I'm sure I'll think of something. Right now, you'd better get back to sleep. I don't want you to miss out because you're not ready." Tophet resumed swinging the watch.

Heather lay back and stared at the watch for only a moment before closing her eyes. She returned to a deep sleep.

"They look so peaceful when they sleep. If only they could always be that content."

Death reappeared and put a finger under Tophet's chin, making her look at him. "I know you'd like to spare them from hardships, but you can't and shouldn't. They'd never overcome anything that way. They'd never learn to appreciate the wonderful joys of life enough to work for them."

She smiled into his eyes. "Like us. We'd never know the joy of love if we hadn't overcome our silly little differences."

"I wonder if we would have ever known it was possible without two annoying mortals crashing into our well-ordered existence and giving us a chance to rediscover how right we are for each other."

"So, did you go to the Goddess?"

"No, I just stormed off and pouted. Sorry."

He pulled her to him until her forehead rested against his, and he stroked her cheek with one finger. A bright greenish light glowed from deep in his eyes. She wrapped her arms around his neck and kissed him with a passion and fervor she hadn't offered for centuries.

"I don't think I'll ever be bored again, as long as you're around, darling."

Death nodded. "I don't think I will be, either." He looked down at the motionless mortals. "Think we should let them have one last 'Goodbye screw' before they go? Just in case."

She gasped. "Why? What are you going to do to them?"

"I have to be honest. I don't know what kind of shape they'll be in once they get back to their own world."

Tophet slapped her hands over her ears. "Don't tell me. I don't think I could take it." She looked down at them and let a tear slip down her cheek. "Okay. Wake them up and we'll let them have one more fuck for the road."

Death leaned toward her and smirked. "Maybe we should have one too."

"Why? Where are you going?"

"Nowhere, honey. I just love fucking."

Tophet chuckled. "You and I have all of eternity for that."

"You're right, and I intend to take full advantage." Death snapped his fingers, and the mortals woke, yawning and stretching.

Heather looked around. "What happened? Why are we still here?"

"Death and I thought you might want one last visit to the grotto. You still have a few minutes and we'll be right here when you get back."

Blaze said, "Seriously? No voyeurism this time?"

"Absolutely none."

Blaze and Heather looked at each other with raised eyebrows, while grins spread across their faces.

"Just call out to us when you're done."

One puff of smoke later, they were on their way to the darkened grotto.

CHAPTER TWENTY-SIX

Blaze began peeling off his clothes as he was talking. "Heather, my love?"

She adored it when he called her that. "Yes?"

"I don't think we're under the spell anymore, do you?"

"I really doubt it." Heather had her clothing off within seconds and since she wasn't wearing any underwear, she was instantly naked. Naked and chilly. "Remember when she said we were soul mates?"

Blaze's eyes were bulging out of his head as he stared at Heather and tried to jump out of his jeans and sneakers at the same time. He wound up falling in the soft grass and Heather giggled.

When he managed to get the last bit of clothing off, he leaned back on his elbows, nonchalantly patting the ground next to him in invitation. "Yeah. Why does that make you think we're not under her spell anymore?"

Heather lay in the grass next to Blaze. His dick was straight and hard, perfect for fondling. "Because it wouldn't do anything."

"You mean it would be redundant?"

"Exactly. So why did you think we might still be affected?"

He leaned over and kissed her hard. "Because you turn me on so damn much. I just want to fuck you every time I look at your ass, your breasts, that luscious trim."

"Fuck away!"

Blaze grinned and fixed his mouth firmly to her breast. Drawing in her nipple, he suckled deeply, and she moaned, ecstatic. The combined heat and suction from his mouth made her wish he had two of them. She imagined he could suck her all the way to orgasm repeatedly without even touching her clit. As he paid thorough attention to one breast with his mouth, he rubbed, squeezed, and massaged the other. Just playing with and sucking her tits made her womb clench, nearly sending her over the edge.

"Oh, my God. I love it when you do that, Blaze. I bet if you touched my clit right now, I'd come."

As if trying to drive her crazy, he barely touched her with a feather-light tap. She arched her back, moaning louder. "Please honey, please. I need to come. I can feel it. I'm right there."

Blaze lifted his mouth off her breast, breaking the much-loved suction only long enough to transfer his attention to the other breast. He attached himself to her nipple and devoured that one just as completely. While he was doing that, he teased her mercilessly by stroking her labia and then inserting his fingers into her soaking wet channel.

"Blaze, I mean it! Get me off, right now!"

He let her breast pop out of his mouth and grinned at her. "Look who's become all assertive. Do you want me to suck you?"

"Yes."

"Say it."

"For God's sake...Suck me, fuck me, make me scream."

Blaze withdrew his fingers and scooted to the vee between her thighs. He parted her lips and licked her clit. Once. Twice. She erupted on three. Shaking and quivering all over, she screamed out the best release of the day.

When inhalation was possible, she lay panting like a race dog as she attempted a look at his cock.

Blaze saw the movement of her eyes and glanced down. He was fully erect, its color deepening. "I'm ready if you are, sweetheart."

Heather spread her legs wide and reached for him. Blaze smiled and poised himself at her opening. In the same teasing way, he poked in a tiny bit and then withdrew. He inserted his shaft a little bit further and eased it back out again, driving her just slightly crazy.

"Damn it, Blaze. Will you please push your cock all the way in and start fucking already?"

He laughed. "I'm always happy to oblige a lady."

Their mutual rhythm started slowly with eyes burning into each other, but it soon took on a life of its own. They were shivering and quivering, shaking and quaking, shuddering and fluttering—soon they were bucking and pow! Massive orgasms rocked both of them. Heather felt it right down to her toenails. Not bad for a 'good little girl'.

***

After a long, languorous kiss, Death rested his head against Tophet's forehead and looked deeply into her eyes. "Are you sure you want me to go to the Goddess without you?"

Tophet ran her hands over his robe, feeling the muscular chest beneath. "I trust you. I don't trust her as far as I can poof her, but I'm sure you're assertive and will tell her, 'No, means no.'"

"She has the Sun God from what I hear, but I don't think they get together very often. That's got to be tough on a relationship."

"It's okay," Tophet said. "Go. Do what you have to do."

"I'll be back in a flash." With that, he kissed her and vanished.

She materialized her fainting couch and had barely settled onto it when a bolt of lightning hit the bank of the pond. Death came running out of the crack in the atmosphere. Surprised, Tophet jumped up and stared at his mussed hair and crooked cape.

"Good and merciful beyond! What happened?"

"I'm sorry," Death panted. "I didn't mean to alarm you."

He hobbled around, rubbing his side as if he had a cramp.

"Are you all right?"

"Yeah, I'm fine. I got her to tell me what I needed to know. It turns out it's up to me anyway, so it's a good thing I went despite the downward turn of the conversation after that."

"What on earth did she say?"

"Oh, that she misses me and thinks about me..."

"Oh, that's just great! Why can't she think about her Sun God?"

"If you'll be quiet and listen to me for a second..."

Tophet crossed her arms and frowned. "Of course. Please finish what you were saying."

Death leaned over and rested his hands on his thighs as he took in a couple more deep breaths. Then he stood and sauntered over to her. "I said I couldn't stay and that it was likely

I wouldn't be visiting at all anymore—because I'm hopelessly and eternally in love with you. Then she kicked me out, literally." He rubbed his right hip and grimaced.

"Oh, honey…" Tophet placed her hands gently on either side of his face. "Thank goodness she didn't get you in the balls."

"She was aiming for them, believe me. I managed to turn and run at the last second. It's a good thing she's an old crone now. She might have caught up with me in one of her younger forms."

"My poor baby," Tophet crooned and kissed him on the nose.

"I'll let you make it up to me later." He looked at his watch. "Right now, I have to get to the lovebirds."

"Are they finished?"

"They'd better be. We only have a few minutes."

"Then go! What are you waiting for?"

Death disappeared in a puff of smoke and returned within seconds. The mortals lay on the bank, just as out of it as before, with Death bent over them.

"What—?" Tophet started.

"Hold on, I have to concentrate. The timing is critical!"

Tophet held her tongue and watched as the couple cuddled close together. She imagined it might not be solely for warmth but also for support. This was bound to be a helluva ride. At Death's touch, they disappeared.

"You did it!" she cried.

"Not yet, but I'm about to." He crossed over to the very edge of the pond and looked up at the sky. "Right about now, a small boat is sinking in the Bermuda triangle. The mayday has been sent out to the Coast Guard and two people are clinging to a single life preserver. They're shivering with hypothermia and their hands are slipping from their death grip on that one and only floating object.

Tophet's hands flew to her mouth.

A moment later, two rubbery ovals dropped out of the sky and Death leaped into the air toward them. He grabbed them in one hand and flung them both back in the direction from whence they came. A second before he would have hit the water, he poofed back to the safety of the bank.

Tophet jammed her hands on her hips. "You didn't!"

Death shrugged and strolled toward her. "I did. It was the only way."

"A near death experience? Are you mad?"

"They'll be talking about it for years. It's perfect. Don't you see?"

"You could have missed! What if you caught only one and not the other?"

"But I didn't."

"But you could have. You haven't done many of those one-at-a-time never mind two-at -once."

Death threw his hands in the air. "I don't believe it. I did what you asked, got rid of the mortals and returned them to their world. They're fine. In fact, they're even better off than before."

"Wait a minute. How do you know what I did for them?"

A newspaper appeared, hanging in the air, and Death shook it open. "It's right here." He read the headline out loud. "Miss Georgia Rescued off Atlantic Coast."

Tophet ripped the newspaper from his grasp. "Give me that."

She pulled a pair of glasses from her robe and set them on her nose. "A daring off-shore rescue by the Coast Guard saved the reigning Miss Georgia, Heather Tripp, and her fiancé, drummer for the successful rock band, Replacement Doors, Blaze Stevens. According to Miss Tripp, if it wasn't for her fiancé, urging her to hold onto the life preserver they shared, she would have sunk to the ocean floor like she had an anchor on her foot. She said it was the power of love, support, and shared memories as well as hopes and dreams for the future that kept them afloat until the Coast Guard arrived. A Coast Guard spokesperson said they thought they were too late, but both responded to CPR and came around quickly."

Death folded his arms looking smug.

"I'm sorry I doubted you," Tophet said.

He kissed her on the forehead. "I'm just happy that it worked out for all of us. Look, it's been an exhausting day. Why don't you lie down and take a nap while I catch up on some of the work I've missed?"

"We both have work to catch up on, but why don't we do it tomorrow? Do you think you might be in the mood for a cuddle?"

As soon as their four-poster bed appeared, they dropped onto it in exhaustion. Tophet settled into Death's arms and wiggled into the comfort of the soft, pillowy, feather bed. With a smile on her face, she closed her eyes and immediately drifted off to sleep.

She couldn't be sure if a voice interrupted her slumber for a moment, or if she had been dreaming, but she could have sworn she heard Heather's voice resonating all around her, saying, "Thank you, Tophet. We won't forget."

Tophet opened her eyes and said, "You're welcome, sweetheart. I won't forget you, either."

She rolled toward Death and felt a lump under her hip. Digging underneath her, she pulled her boomerang out and smiled. "I'll miss them."

Death brushed her hair away from her face and kissed her. "Maybe they'll come back someday."

Tophet chuckled and snuggled into his embrace. "They all do."

Ashlyn Chase describes herself as an Almond Joy bar; a little nutty, a little flaky, but sweet, wanting only to give readers satisfying stories that leave them smiling.

She worked as an RN for 20 years but retired early to write full-time. She is a multi-published, award-winning author of paranormal romantic comedies.

She lives in Florida with her true superhero husband whom she calls Mr. Amazing and two loveable cats.

Website www.ashlynchase.com
Join my Facebook fan page: https://www.facebook.com/Auth
orAshlynChase
Follow me on Bookbub: https://www.bookbub.com/authors
/ashlyn-chase
Instagram https://www.instagram.com/ashlynlaughin/
Pinterest https://www.pinterest.com/ashlynchase/

www.ingramcontent.com/pod-product-compliance
Lightning Source LLC
Chambersburg PA
CBHW021446150726
47989CB00001B/422